LOCALS

ONLY

BY

PETE BIRLE

Scobre Press Corporation
2255 Calle Clara
La Jolla, CA 92037

Scobre Press books may be purchased for
educational, business or sales promotional use.

Edited by Helen Glenn Court
Illustrated by Gail Piazza
Cover Design by Michael Lynch
Skateboard Content Consultant, Patrick McGinn

ISBN# 1-933423-44-7

HOME RUN EDITION

www.scobre.com

CHAPTER ONE

GERMANY

Thwomp!

As soon as my foot connected with the ball, I knew it was a goal. I don't know if anyone else knew it, but I did.

A year earlier, I wouldn't have been so sure. Things had changed a lot since then. All of a sudden, I had become an offensive threat. I no longer doubted what I could do on the soccer field. Especially when it came to scoring.

Basically, I had game. I just hoped I wasn't the only one who noticed it.

My name is Toby Hardin. Back then, I was a 13-year-old seventh grader—the son of a U.S. Air Force officer living in Ramstein, Germany. Sure, growing up in Europe meant that I played a lot of soccer. But being Colonel Hardin's boy had more to do with my progress on the field. I was a focused kid, and I wanted to be the best I could be. This drive to succeed was something my father had demanded of me. Early on, I learned that when Colonel Hardin gave an order, you followed it.

I had my game face on that day. After all, it was the tryouts for the Ramstein Rottweilers—the best youth team in the area. I was pretty sure my spot on the roster was a lock. I had played on the team for a few years already. But I wanted more than to just stay on the squad. My goal was to be a starter. If this happened, I'd be the only American on the field at the start of every game.

That's why, after taking a pass near the 18, I was thinking shot. It was time I showed these Europeans what I could do.

I knew the defender who was guarding me was leaning right. I sensed I had him beat. There was no reason to wait. One touch was all I needed. I pushed the ball out so I could strike it with my left foot. The goalkeeper didn't expect me to go left, much less shoot. Because of that, he was out of position. I had a clear shot on goal.

Without breaking stride, I slammed the ball. The force of my kick did the rest. It spun toward the upper corner of the net, where no goalie could reach it. As the ball banged into the cords, several of my teammates screamed: "Goooaaaal!" My heart raced, and I pumped my fist in the air. There was nothing quite like scoring.

After getting a few chest bumps, I ran to the sideline. Taking a drink of water, I stared out onto the field from alongside the bench. Sweat was pouring down my forehead and running into my eyes. It was unusually hot for August in Germany. But I didn't have time to worry about the weather. I had a tryout to finish. Besides, I was from Texas. I knew a little bit about hot summers.

"Toby! Get back out there," Coach Landeck shouted to me in English. "Schnell, schnell. Quickly, quickly," he added. "And move to center half."

"Ja," I said in German, before expanding my answer in English. "Center half."

It still felt weird when I spoke German. I know it must have sounded even weirder to those around me. Hearing a Texan speak in German is pretty hard on the ears. I had arrived in Ramstein six years earlier and ever since had tried to lose my Texas accent. I wasn't making any headway. In fact, my efforts actually backfired. Karl, my best friend, said my Germexan accent made me sound like I came from another planet.

I ran back out to take my spot in the middle of the field. I took in a few deep breaths. Coach Landeck had never put me at center midfield— the playmaker's spot. I was a little nervous. Playing center mid is like being the quarterback in football. If you play the position correctly, you'll have the ball most of the time. Center mid is usually where the best—and smartest— athlete plays. Needless to say, I was excited about this opportunity.

It didn't take long for me to show Coach he'd made a good choice. I picked up a loose ball deep on my team's side of the field. Then I set up our advance. Pushing forward, I shouted encouragement to my teammates. I didn't give away my intentions, though. The only thing the other team knew was that I was in control.

As a result, two defenders double-teamed me at midfield. I knew right away that someone was open. I kept the ball close as the two defenders closed in. I gave a quick nod over to Karl at center forward. This signal let him know I needed him to come back for the ball.

Karl picked up on my hint right away. This was the benefit of us having played together for several years. As he approached the two defenders from behind, I put my toe under the ball. Then I chipped it. I watched as it arched like a rainbow over the defenders' heads. So did they.

Caught off-guard, the two of them stood flat-footed. I broke for the goal. In the meantime, Karl positioned himself under the pass. Turning his head, he waited for the ball to come down. When it did, he bumped it my way with his head, a perfect wall pass. By the time I received the ball, I had left those defenders in the dust.

After trapping Karl's return, I dribbled once before lofting a pass down the sideline. The ball was slightly ahead of a streaking winger. He caught up to it on a bounce and launched a half-volley at the net. The goalie never had a chance.

I smiled when I heard the shouts again—"Goooaaaal!"

After Karl and I gave each other a chest bump, we headed for the bench. As existing Rottweiler players, we were done "trying out" for the day. We both smiled, feeling as though we had proved something.

I guzzled some water and thought about my performance that afternoon. Sure, I felt secure about my place on the team, but now I wondered: Was I the Rottweilers' new center midfielder? I soon found out.

Coach Landeck came over and put his hand on my shoulder. "Toby," he said. "I've seen enough. You're my new starting center half." Coach smiled his crooked smile. "It's your time now, G.I. Joe."

I had been in Germany since I was 7 years old. That's when the Hardins—Dad, Mom and I—left America. We were living in San Antonio, Texas, at Lackland Air Force Base. Texas was where I had been born and the place I considered home.

As far as military "brats" go, I had it pretty good. Most kids with a parent in the armed forces moved every year or so. I'd only had two stops in 13 years, the last six at Ramstein Air Base.

My dad was already a colonel when we first made our home in western Germany. Even though we had been here for a while, I still considered myself a Texan. I was a cowboy in Germany—talk about a fish out of water! It wasn't easy for me to adjust when I first arrived. I couldn't get used to the winters and all that snow. There isn't much of the white stuff in southern Texas. I couldn't get used to the food, either. There was bratwurst, bockwurst, knackwurst, weisswurst. Man, just give me a hot dog! Plus, I couldn't get good barbecue anywhere! That took some serious getting used to.

And, finally, saying "y'all" just wasn't cutting it.

Granted, I went to an American school right on the base. But I was with the locals all the time, which was how my parents wanted it. It's also how Karl Von Hirsch and I came to be best buddies.

We hit it off because of soccer and because our dads were in the service. Karl's father was a German military officer based at Ramstein. We were products of a military lifestyle—with all the discipline and competitiveness. We were serious kids, with dirty blond buzz cuts and good manners. We approached everything like the Air Force motto, "Aim High."

This was especially true when it came to soccer. I had played junior league soccer in Texas as a young boy. The sport was growing back home, but it still lagged behind baseball, basketball and football. When I moved to Germany, my love for soccer became an obsession. As it turned out, the entire country was soccer-crazy. The sport helped me accept, if not embrace, my new home.

Our team—the Rottweilers—had largely been together for the past few years. We were good. I had always been an average player on this team of young European stars. Then I hit a growth spurt and things started changing. Now, I was moving into the starting lineup—and at center midfield! This coming season was going to be the most important of my life.

As soon as tryouts were over, I hopped on my bicycle. Karl jumped on his, too, and we proceeded to race each other home. Karl and I were forever pushing each other that way. Other kids we knew liked to sit around and play video games. We couldn't relate. Sure, we relaxed every once in a while. But the rest of the time, we'd go for it, whatever "it" happened to be.

Because our families lived on the same street, Karl and I had daily races home. On that day, Karl got the best of me by a few feet.

Saying goodbye to him, I had no idea how my life was about to change. Karl pedaled over to his house, and I stuck my bike in the garage. Right away, I could sense that something was wrong. Usually, Mom would have dinner on the stove. She'd be outside watering the flower boxes that lined the windowsills of our house. Sometimes she'd even be singing. Plus, I'd see my dad through the window, in his easy chair.

Today, there were no smells coming from the

kitchen. Nobody was outside, and the living room curtains were closed. I walked through the door slowly. Mom was sitting across from Dad at the kitchen table. Our eyes met as I shut the door. She looked as though she had been crying. Dad was in full uniform, too, which was strange for a Saturday. He stood at attention when I entered the room. His silver colonel's eagle shone brightly on his collar.

"Sit down, Toby," he said.

I did. "What's the matter?" I asked. "Am I in trouble?"

"No," Mom said. "Of course not."

"I have some news," Dad said. He sat down in the seat across from me and looked right into my eyes. Then he spoke like he always did—in a strong and clear voice. He would make no apologies for what he was about to say. "I've resigned my commission in the Air Force. We're moving back home."

My heart began to race. "What?" I asked, caught completely unaware.

"We're heading back to the States, Toby."

I looked over at my mother and then back at my dad. This was just like him to make a big decision without asking me. Or Mom.

I could tell that Mom just found out, too. It was also clear that her first reaction was to shed a few tears. I don't think it was so much that Mom was unhappy about moving back home. She just would have liked to have been a part of the decision. In truth,

I felt the same way.

Six years earlier, when we learned Dad was being transferred to Germany, it was similar. It was a done deal by the time word got to Mom and me. Pack up your boots and spurs, we're heading across the ocean. No discussion. No complaining. And certainly no vote. It was the same thing once again. Only this time, the Air Force didn't make the decision. Dad did.

"Are we going back to Texas?" I asked. I had never expected to see San Antonio again when we first left the States. Moving back to Texas wouldn't be all that bad. After all, I was a native Texan—raised there for half my life. It might be cool to reunite with some of my old pals, too.

A tiny smile started to form at the corners of my mouth. And then ...

"No, son, not to Texas. We're moving to Florida."

"Florida?" I asked. "What's in Florida?"

"My new job," my father answered. He walked into the living room and plopped down in his chair.

I followed him. "What job?" I asked.

"I'll be working at New Piper Aircraft in Vero Beach." Dad said. Then, he reached into his briefcase and pulled out a blue folder.

He handed it to me, and I opened it. Inside was information about my new life, Dad's new job and our new town. It was delivered to me like I was about to go on a military mission. The folder was marked

"Operation Florida: Toby." I looked over at Mom. I noticed she had a similar folder stuck under her arm.

I flipped through pages and pages of information. Dad didn't know how to operate any other way than this. My new life would begin without emotion. I had been briefed by the Colonel. I had been given the information. And now I was expected to deal with it.

Dad looked up at me, smiling. "You know, Toby, Vero Beach is the winter home of the Los Angeles Dodgers. They call it Dodgertown. And we're not going to be far from the ballpark."

"Is that so?" I asked, faking interest. "I guess I'll be able to catch some games, then." As if I wanted to watch baseball. I didn't care about baseball.

I continued to look through the information he had provided. There were maps, photos of my new school and a list of area soccer camps. There were also newspaper articles about nearby restaurants and beaches.

"Will we be living in Vero Beach?" I asked.

"No," my dad answered. "We're going to be just up the road, in a town called Sebastian. It's known as one of the best surfing spots on the East Coast. It's all in your folder."

"Wow, baseball *and* surfing. Am I lucky or what?" The sarcasm dripped off my words. There was no hiding it. I had no interest in either Dodgertown or Surf City. And I had just made it clear to my dad.

"I know you're not thrilled to hear this, Toby,"

my dad said, standing up. "But you better watch your tone, Airman."

He always called me Airman when he was lecturing me. I'm sure he did it to all the men under his command. I was used to it, but I didn't like it.

"Did you think we were going to live in Germany the rest of our lives?" *His* voice had a hint of sarcasm in it now.

"No," I said. "I'm just not happy knowing I'll never get to play on my soccer team again. Especially since I'm going to be starting at center half."

Just saying these words made my lip tremble. I had finally achieved my goal of starting for the Rottweilers. But, just like that, it had been taken away from me. I took a deep breath to hold back my tears.

"That's wonderful, news, Toby," Mom said. "Congratulations."

She looked over at my father, but he didn't respond. So, after a moment or two of awkward silence, she spoke up again.

"What about Karl, sweetheart?" She stroked the back of my head. "Aren't you going to miss him, too?"

"I'm trying not to think about never seeing my best friend again," I said. I gave Mom a reassuring look. "I'm not happy about it at all."

"That's understandable," my father replied. "But the world is a lot smaller than it used to be. I'm sure Karl would like to visit Florida some day. You can always take a trip back here, too. Planes can fly across the ocean in only few hours. Check your briefing. I've actually included a photo of the new Airbus we're flying to Florida in. It's a beautiful aircraft, Toby."

That was Dad's way of trying to offer support—with some advice about air travel. He totally missed the point.

I located the picture of the commercial jet in my packet. "It's a cool plane, Dad," I said quietly, barely looking up at him. "When do we leave?"

"In a week."

"Great," I answered. "I wasn't sure if I'd get a chance to say goodbye to Karl."

I tossed the folder down on the coffee table in front of my father. Then I left, slamming my bedroom door behind me.

CHAPTER TWO

SEBASTIAN

Dad told me to think of this the same way he did every assignment he'd ever been given. "This is an adventure," he told me as we boarded the plane. "You don't have to forget your soccer team or Karl. You just have to move on."

"Yes sir."

A few hours earlier, Karl and I had said our farewells in true military fashion. Neither of us cried. Just a handshake, a smile and a "see ya around." Dramatic goodbyes weren't going to get me anywhere. Even before Dad spoke on the airplane, I had been preparing myself to move on.

It had been a week since Dad dropped the bomb on me. It took some time, but I was warming up to the idea of returning home. It had been a while since I had been in the United States. I had a new mission now, and I was ready to accept it.

As the plane took off, I kept reading through my materials. Dad had also given me a stack of magazines that morning. I was curious. This was my new life, and I didn't know anything about it.

First, I learned that Sebastian, Florida, offers some of the best surfing in the world. This is in part due to the great weather, beautiful scenery and warm water. But mostly it's because it has one of the most consistent surf breaks anywhere. In fact, Sebastian Inlet is where some of the world's greatest surfers began their careers.

I read on, as the topic quickly changed from surfing to fishing. Every September, hundreds of snook fishermen descend on Sebastian in their boats. As a result, the inlet gets pretty crowded.

Surfing and fishing and crowds of people on boats. Wonderful, I said to myself, shaking my head from side to side.

I then turned to another magazine, *Florida Trend*. I came across an article about an activity that was rivaling surfing among Sebastian's youth. It was taking over the town and the neighboring communities. It was skateboarding, a sport I knew next to nothing about it. *At least it's on land,* I thought.

Skateboarding became popular way back in the 1950s. California surfers were looking for something to do when the waves were flat. The fad didn't last long, though. By 1965, skateboarding was more or less dead. The so-called sport and its freestyle creativity had disappeared by the mid-1960s. Parts for the wooden decks were hard to find, and the clay wheels were dangerous and hard to control.

In 1972, the urethane wheel appeared. This sparked new interest in skateboarding. By the mid-1970s, the sport took a big step. A contest was held in Del Mar, California, as part of the Ocean Festival. It was won by the Zephyr (or Z) team, known also as the Lords of Dogtown. People began to see that skateboarding could be much more than just a hobby. It could be a serious—yet somewhat underground and radical—sport.

Then, in 1978, Alan "Ollie" Gelfand invented a maneuver that gave skateboarding new life. Gelfand would slam his back foot down on the tail of his board and jump, popping himself and his board into the air. The *ollie* was born.

The sport gained popularity with the arrival of teenage pro Tony Hawk in the 1980s. It took off again in 1995, thanks to the arrival of the X-Games. It's now—to the dismay of many pro skaters—mainstream. Today, *halfpipes* and *pools* are popping up all over America in places called skateboard parks. Apparently, there was a really big one in Sebastian.

The article went on about how popular skateboarding had become in Florida's beach towns. Many kids were skateboarding even when the waves were breaking. They had traded in their surfboards for skateboards. With their long hair, baggy pants and woolen hats, they vowed never to wax again.

I closed the magazine and stared out the airplane window. All of a sudden, I wasn't so excited about my mission. Baseball, surfing and fishing seemed like afterthoughts in Sebastian. Skateboarding was king.

"Bummer, dude!" I said out loud.

I saw them on the steps of Indian River Middle School. And I thought they looked like clowns.

It was my first day in my new school. I didn't know their names, and I didn't care. They seemed like a pair of slackers to me. They were the kind of kids who represented everything my military background fought against.

Craig "Grommet" Pedersen was the leader of the duo. He had straight, blond hair that went down to his shoulders. I found out later he was trying to look like original Z-Boy Stacy Peralta. He helped to pioneer today's skate-punk scene. I thought Pedersen looked ridiculous. I couldn't help running my hand over my buzz cut as I walked by.

Next to him was Dane "Hot Dog" Armour. Dane got this nickname because his last name was the same as the frankfurter company. But he also got it because of his attitude on a skateboard. He had a head of bushy brown hair. It was mostly hidden, though, beneath a red woolen hat (a beanie, in skate-speak). He wore it despite the fact it was nearly 90 degrees.

Both of them dressed like they had gotten their

clothes from the local thrift shop. I only paid attention to them because they were hard to ignore. Plus, it was my first day in a new school—in a "new" country. I wanted to get the lay of the land.

They noticed me, too, as I made my way toward the school's front door.

"Hey, Shubee!" called Pedersen. "Where's your surfboard?"

At first, I didn't know his question was directed at me. But it didn't take me long to realize I was the shubee. A shubee is someone who "dresses surf" but has never tried surfing. From the looks of my clothes, I was the king of shubees. My tropical shirt and cargo shorts said I was trying too hard to fit in. In short, I was.

I made it through that first day, despite my clothes. After last period, I was thrilled it was over. The next step was to find the school soccer coach. This was a really big deal for me. I was sure that, once again, soccer would help me make friends and fit in.

I found Coach Pappas in the equipment room, off to the side of the gym. He was stuffing soccer balls into a huge bag.

"Excuse me, sir, but are you Coach Pappas?"

An athletic man in his late 30s turned to face me. He was wearing a green T-shirt with a turtle on it. "Yes, I'm Coach Pappas," he added, not bothering to look up. "Who are you, and what can I do for you?"

"I'm Toby Hardin, and I'm in eighth grade," I said. "My folks and I just moved here from Germany. I played a lot of soccer there. I was hoping I could try out for the team here."

Coach Pappas began to size me up. His eyes traveled from my head down to my feet and then back up again. Then he stared directly at my face. "Germany, huh? Played a lot of soccer over there, did you?"

"Yes sir, I did. Right before I moved, I made the starting lineup on my team in Ramstein."

"Is that right?" he asked, his eyes beginning to sparkle. "What position?"

"Center mid," I replied with a smile.

At that, his eyes turned on like light bulbs in a dark room. "You were a starting center half on a team full of Germans?" he asked. The disbelief was evident in his voice.

Coach Pappas stopped stacking cones. You could see the wheels beginning to turn in his head. He looked like someone who just pulled the winning lottery ticket out of his pocket. "We could certainly use a center half with European soccer experience," said Coach Pappas. He reached out and shook my hand.

"I was hoping you could," I said. "When can I try out for the team?"

"Don't worry about that," he continued, his mind racing. "Stop by practice in a half hour on the field behind the school. You can meet your teammates."

"So I'm on the team?" I asked with surprise in

my voice. "No tryout?"

"You're on it," he said. "This is your official invitation to join the Green Turtles. It's not every day we get a center midfielder from Europe looking to join us. Soccer is big here, Hardin, but not as big as surfing and skateboarding," he continued. "Kids here would rather spend their time on one kind of a board or another. Some of the parents actually have to *make* their kids play soccer. You, on the other hand, want to play," he said. "So, you'll play."

I didn't know what to say. I couldn't imagine having to be forced to play soccer. And yet, I recalled my father saying something to me when I was much younger. About how he was going to sign me up for sports. As I thought back, it became clearer. I even remembered my dad's words. "Team sports will provide you with leadership and experience in a challenging environment," he said.

It's a good thing I took to it, given that I didn't have a choice. For some reason, I thought back to those two skateboarders I had seen earlier. I wondered why they had chosen skateboarding over baseball or soccer. Then I wondered why I was even thinking about those guys.

Coach Pappas interrupted my thoughts. "You should head over to the field," he said. "I just have to make sure everything's okay with you joining the team. I'll see you at practice."

Twenty-six minutes later, I watched as the Indian River Green Turtles warmed up. They were actually pretty good. The guys were playing a half-field scrimmage. No, they weren't the Rottweilers. But I could tell right away that they knew how to play.

One more thing was clear, too. And this was the most important one to me. I would fit in just fine with the Green Turtles. I could see myself providing the link between the offense and defense. I could be this team's starting center midfielder! Not only that, but I might even be its star. I grinned. The move to Florida was turning out to be somewhat positive. I decided that helping bring the Green Turtles a championship would be my new goal.

Just then, a hand landed on my shoulder. It belonged to Coach Pappas. I looked up at him. He wasn't smiling anymore. In fact, he had a sad look on his face. "Bad news, Toby," he said quietly.

I gulped. "What do you mean, Coach?"

"You can't play," he said. "At least not this year."

"Why not? My mom registered me. I'm an official student here," I pleaded.

"I know, but it's not that simple," said the coach. "The school year and the fall sports season have already begun. Because you're coming to us from another district, you have to sit out this season. I wish it weren't the case, but it's the policy," he said. "There's nothing I can do, Toby."

I looked out at the Green Turtles. They were

running, dribbling, passing and shooting their way around the soccer field. I should have been out there with them. Who knows, I might have even been elected captain, another dream of mine.

"This is just great," I said, "just great."

"I'm sorry, son," Coach Pappas repeated. "There's always next year. You can play on the freshman team when you get to high school. I guess my loss will be their gain."

I nodded before turning and walking away.

When I had escaped from view, I yelled at the top of my lungs. "Thanks, Dad!" I hoped he could hear me all the way in his office in Vero Beach.

I turned the corner for the teacher's parking lot, where I had chained my bike. I noticed the skateboarding duo who greeted me upon my arrival that day. *This day is just getting better and better.* I shook my head. The last thing I needed right now was to be hassled by these two.

I watched them as I passed, making sure not to stare. I stole a few glances while I unlocked my bike. Luckily, they were too busy practicing their stunts to make fun of me again.

They had turned the pavement of the parking lot into their own skateboard park. I had no idea what the tricks they were doing were called. But they looked awesome. Not only that, but they seemed really hard. I was amazed at what they were able to do. They seemed to defy gravity. To be honest, I was surprised that these two scrubs were such great athletes.

It was hard for me to understand Pederson and Armour. On the one hand, they spun, flipped and basically flew in the air. I could relate to their focus and desire to push the limits of their sport. On the other hand, I could almost hear my father's voice inside my head. *Those jokers lack teamwork and they dress like slobs. Always present yourself in a way that demands others' respect, Airman.* Yup, I knew exactly what Colonel Hardin would think of these slackers.

After taking one last look, I unchained my bike, hopped on it and headed home.

CHAPTER THREE

TWO OF A KIND

I learned that there was a recreational soccer league in Sebastian. At first, I was excited. Until, that is, I talked to one of the guys on the middle-school team. Coach Pappas didn't like his players joining traveling teams during the season, so most didn't. The rec league was made up of players not good enough to make the Green Turtles. Although I was dying to play soccer, I wasn't interested in joining the "B" team. After all, I had been a budding star in Germany just a few weeks earlier.

Instead of complaining, I set a goal to make the freshman team the next fall. In the meantime, I would have to stay in shape. My training program was designed, of course, with the help of my father. It was tough, but it was also short. That left plenty of time for the other things I liked to do. I just hadn't figured out what those things were yet.

My father offered a solution to my boredom problem: a job. "Nothing wrong with a 14-year-old learning responsibility and the value of a dollar."

"But I'm only 13, Dad," I reminded him. I wasn't thrilled about the idea of working.

"Only until tomorrow," he replied. "It's time to grow up, Airman."

Some happy birthday, I thought to myself.

My dad knew someone who owned one of the food stands at the beach. And he needed a kid to work weekends. So, on the day after my birthday, I became an employee at Dex's Snack Shack.

Dex's served hamburgers, hot dogs and fried fish sandwiches to hungry beachgoers, surfers and fishermen. According to the locals, Dex's made the best burger on the Florida coast. Even in winter, there were always surfers and fisherman in need of a quick bite. That's why Cliff Dexter—an ex-Navy cook known as Dex—hired several neighborhood kids. He needed the help during the weekend lunch rush.

By the end of my first day at Dex's, I had settled into a groove. I put my work ethic to the test as a fast-food employee. I filled cups with soda, scooped ice cream and kept the counter spotless. It was tiring, but it felt good to earn money for a job well done. And the view from Dex's was awesome! Between customers, I would stare out at the Atlantic Ocean and watch the surfers.

I often saw those two skateboarders from school, too. They spent every weekend on the board-walk in front of Dex's, doing their thing. At one point, Pedersen noticed I had been staring at him. When our eyes met, he did the strangest thing. He winked at me.

Now, I wasn't too comfortable being winked at. That much was for sure. Still, it was much better than being made fun of. I didn't get the impression that he was goofing on me, either. It was like he realized I had been watching and appreciating his skills.

For a moment, I thought I might like to try skate-boarding myself. This idea passed as quickly as it had come into my head. After all, I was, in just about every way, the opposite of a skater. This so-called sport was for other kids. You know, the kids who break the rules. I was a team player, an Air Force colonel's son.

I followed the rules because I knew the rules were there to help me. My upbringing did not reward you for being different, or going off on your own. I had been taught to follow instructions. No individual is greater than the team. This philosophy had been fed to me since I was in diapers. I believed it in my soul.

Still, the moves of Pedersen and Armour were amazing. But the lack of teamwork, rules, coaches and strategy made me uncomfortable. Skateboarding went against everything I had bought into my entire life. Still, I didn't need a superior officer to tell me that watching it felt good.

After only a few weekends at Dex's, I graduated to the grill. I made fries and cooked the burgers people lined up for. Dex said if I kept it up, he'd always have a job for me. He told me he liked my leadership skills. By setting an example, I made everyone around me push it a bit harder.

All that was great, I told him. Still, I wished I could put in more hours than he was giving me. Because Dex only needed me on the weekends, I still had a lot of free time on my hands. I was a good student, and homework was never a problem for me. And, though intense, Dad's conditioning program only took 30 minutes a day.

Being the new kid, I didn't have any friends in Florida. I spent a lot of time alone those first few weeks. When I wasn't reading, working or doing schoolwork, I was kicking a soccer ball. Usually, it was against the garage door. I needed something more to keep me busy.

To avoid the boredom, I started hanging out down at the beach more. I'd head down on my bike to ride along the boardwalk. It seemed that every time I was there, I'd see those two skateboarders. After a few days, I started watching them more closely. I sat on a bench about 20 yards away and stared. I studied their every move. Although I wouldn't have admitted it, I was drawn to skateboarding in a powerful way. Nothing had ever pulled at me like this before. Not even soccer.

At night, I would go online and look at skate-boarding websites. I'd watch video clips to learn more about the tricks I'd seen earlier that day. For starters, there were ollies, *manuals*, *indygrabs* and *shovits*. Pederson and Armour pulled off these moves easily, usually in front of a crowd of onlookers.

When things slowed down at Dex's, I'd scope out the action from behind the counter. Just as I had been with soccer, I was obsessed. Still, I didn't admit my interest to anyone, especially my father.

Although we weren't in any classes together, I always ran into Craig Pedersen at school. Nearly every day, he gave a skateboard demonstration after lunch. He was like a local celebrity. He and I never spoke those first few weeks of school. Several times, Craig would catch me staring at him as he skated near the playground. And each time he did, he'd give me that wink. Of course, I would look away. I was intimidated by the kid who turned recess into his own private skateboard demo.

What I didn't know, however, was that Craig often watched me on the playground, too. When I wasn't staring at him, I juggled a soccer ball. I'd bounce it off my feet, thighs and head. Soon, I was up to 85 touches without letting the ball fall to the ground. I often drew a small crowd myself.

What I didn't realize was that Craig had become one of my biggest fans. By watching me, he was getting a good look at my drive to be the best. I was never satisfied with juggling the ball, say, 70 times. If I hit that milestone on a Tuesday, by Wednesday I'd be shooting for 75.

I wasn't trying to be the best so others could give me attention. I wanted to be the best I could be for *me*. I had a genuine desire to perform at the top of my ability. It's what my father expected of me, but it's also what I expected of myself. I brought this attitude with me when accomplishing any task, big or small. In watching me from a distance, this quality of mine became obvious to Craig. We didn't know it yet, but we were two of a kind.

One day, Craig approached me. "Hey," he said, walking over from the blacktop onto the grass.

I looked up, surprised to see him in front of me. The ball I had been juggling on my head fell to the ground. Not wanting to be embarrassed, I quickly trapped it under my foot. "Hey," I said, realizing he hadn't called me shubee this time.

"You're pretty good at juggling that ball," he said. "You really concentrate on it."

"Thanks." I was surprised mostly. Why was the resident skateboarding king interested in what I was doing?

"How do you do it?" he asked me. "It looks really hard to master."

"It takes practice," I told him. "I've been play-ing soccer for a long time."

"Do you play on the team?" Craig stared at the

ball beneath my foot.

"No, I just moved here. The school has some weird rule about transfers sitting out a season. It makes no sense." Without thinking, I kicked the ball over to him. It was the same thing I would have done if Karl were there.

Craig looked surprised as the ball rolled over to him, but managed to trap it under his foot. "Can you show me how to juggle?"

"Here?"

"Why not?" He dropped the skateboard he was holding. "If I start now, maybe I can play on the team next year."

I wondered why this skateboarder wanted to learn how to juggle a soccer ball. Still, I began to show him how to do it. To my surprise, he got really into it. Although I could tell he wasn't familiar with the sport, he gave it his all. In fact, he had a focused intensity that reminded me of myself. I was shocked that a skater—one of *those* kids—could be so naturally athletic.

I figured Craig wanted to try juggling because he appreciated the skill involved. I think he also respected the fact that it took some time and effort. I didn't tell him, but that was exactly how I felt watching him skateboard.

The bell rang just as Craig juggled the ball for the eighth time. The noise didn't rattle him. He stayed "in the zone" until the last touch, his 12th. The ball bounced off his head and hit the ground. Craig reached back and kicked a perfect pass to me. Then he picked up his skateboard. "Thanks, dude. But I think I'll stick with this," he said, patting the tool of his trade.

"That looks just as hard to master," I said.

"Harder," he said, heading for the door and fifth period. "You should give it a try some time."

A week went by, and I was at work on a cool Saturday. As I was setting up a tray of hamburger buns alongside the grill, I looked up. Pedersen and Armour were sitting at the end of the counter. Their skateboards were on the ground at their feet. I watched as they dug into their pockets for enough change to buy some fries.

"What can I get for you guys?"

"Just an order of fries," Craig said.

"Coming right up."

"You talk weird, dude," Dane Armour laughed right in my face. He continued, "Aren't you from Austria or something?"

My face turned red as I moved over to stand directly in front of Dane. I hated my accent. In Germany, I sounded like a Texan. Now, in Florida, I apparently sounded like an Austrian. It was enough to drive me crazy! I took a deep breath before responding.

"My dad was in the Air Force, so I lived in Germany for the past six years," I said. "But I'm not

German. I'm from Texas."

"It's Toby, right?" Craig asked, extending his fist. "Dane's just bustin.'"

I bumped knuckles with Craig and then with Dane, who gave me a smile. "I hope you can make fries as good as you can juggle. Craig says you're the man with a soccer ball, Toby."

I relaxed a bit. I had thought I had an enemy in Dane Armour. It was clear now that he was just goofing. And it was funny, actually. Karl used to hassle me about my accent all the time.

"How do you know my name?"

"Dane's in your homeroom, dude," Craig said. The tone of his voice confirmed my question was, indeed, a stupid one.

"Oh yeah," I said. I had forgotten that Dane was one of the first people I saw every morning.

"We always see you watching us skate down here, and at school, too."

I looked down, embarrassed that I was being called out for staring. "Yeah," I said. "You guys are good. I mean, I don't know that much about skateboarding. ..."

Craig interrupted me, "Have you ever ridden?"

"A skateboard?" I asked. "No," I laughed. "I've never ridden anything other than a bike . . . and a horse once."

They laughed. They seemed to think this was hilarious.

31

"So, I guess you don't surf, either, huh, shubee?" asked Dane.

"Nope, not a day in my life," I said. "The clothes were courtesy of my mom. You know how that goes."

"For sure," Dane said.

Craig nodded.

The buzzer behind me went off, meaning that the fries were ready. I put them on the counter in front of Craig. "Thanks, Toby," he said, picking up the fries. As he was leaving, he called over his shoulder. "If you ever want to try skateboarding, let me know."

"Okay, thanks," I said, as Craig and Dane went back to the boardwalk to skate.

Although I was the opposite of a skater in every way, I was drawn to skateboarding. I stared out at the boardwalk. Then I closed my eyes, picturing myself on a board. I was flying through the air with the same ability as Craig and Dane. I smiled as my daydream became clear.

Then I heard a booming voice in my ear. "Hey, kid!" Dex yelled from the other side of the room. "I ain't paying you to stare at the ocean. I got a broom with your name on it. Now let's move!"

CHAPTER FOUR

FLYBOY

I was off the following day. The September rain scared everyone off the beach. When I got to work at 11 that morning, Dex told me to go back home. A storm was passing through. It was supposed to be gone by 3 o'clock. But Dex wasn't going to pay me to "sit around and stare out at sea."

About 2:20, the sun came out. Although the streets were wet, I decided to take a ride on my bike. I flipped on a pair of sunglasses and headed toward the beach. Along the way, I saw two kids coasting toward me on skateboards. I started to smile when I saw it was Craig and Dane. They each had a backpack on and appeared to be on their way someplace. As we approached one another, they slowed down.

"Dex's is closed, brah," said Hot Dog.

"Yeah, I know," I said. "I was just going up to look at the beach."

"The real action is where we're headed now," said Craig.

"Where's that?" I asked.

"Down at the skate park," Craig answered. "Wanna come jam with us?"

"Me?" I asked. "Jam?" My face showed my complete surprise at the invitation.

"You don't have to if you're scared." Dane laughed. I knew he was joking, but his words still stung. Although Craig seemed to like me, I still wasn't sure about Hot Dog Armour.

"Let's go, Craig," Hot Dog continued. "We're burning daylight here."

Craig ignored his friend. "You really should give skateboarding a try," he said, staring at me. It was the same way he had looked at me since I got here. It was as if Craig saw something in me that I couldn't see. Or maybe I did see it and just wasn't ready to admit it.

"I know you want to give it a try, Toby," Craig continued. "I can tell it's killing you." It was as if Craig was in my head.

He was right. I desperately wanted to give skateboarding a try. Still, I didn't respond right away. Hot Dog was right, too. I *was* scared. These guys weren't headed down to a soccer field. They were going to a skate park. There, I would feel like an outsider. It was where *those* kids went to refuse to play by the world's rules. Everything about it went against who I was—or who I thought I was, anyway.

I looked over at Dane. He kicked the side of Craig's board, urging him to move on. "Come on, Craig! He obviously doesn't want to skate. Leave it alone."

Craig didn't flinch. Now my heart was pounding. I knew that this would likely be my last chance to accept his offer.

"Let's do it," I said.

"You are going to love this," Craig smiled as he skated toward the park, yelling over his shoulder to me. "You're never too old to learn how to skate, and there's no better day to start than today."

These two skateboarders—even with their long hair, grunge style and surfer lingo—were okay. They reached out to me, encouraging me to try to *their* sport. That said a lot about them. We rode through the streets of Sebastian—me on a bike, and Craig and Dane on their boards. As we did, we got to know each other better. Best of all was that Dane had accepted the prospect of me skating with him.

The streets dried quickly in the Florida sun. As we pulled up to the park, the sky was clear overhead. Craig and Dane skidded to a halt and threw off their backpacks. They slapped five with some of their buddies. I was sure I had made a mistake coming. I definitely didn't fit in.

I checked out everything—from what clothes

people wore, to what boards they used. After a few minutes, I looked across the park. Craig was talking to a few guys, who were all looking in my direction. Then I heard someone shout, "You gotta learn some time, dude!" A few other guys nodded their head at me.

It was at that moment when something occurred to me. The age-old surf town saying, "Locals Only," didn't seem to apply to these guys. I mean, I didn't look anything like them. I didn't talk anything like them. And I couldn't do the things they could on a skateboard. Yet, I was there to give it a shot, and they respected that.

Everyone was cool except for one guy—Eddie Rios. Rios was older than us, about 18. He had a ponytail, long sideburns and a goatee. He may have had "the look," but I wasn't impressed. In fact, I figured out pretty quickly that he thought he was "the man." He wanted everyone to think of this as *his* skate park.

I watched Craig and Dane gear up, pulling helmets and pads out of their packs. As they did, Craig described the politics at the park. Apparently, Eddie was the unofficial godfather to the young skateboarders in town. He had especially taken a liking to Craig. This was obviously because Craig was the best skateboarder around.

Craig tolerated Eddie because he knew that the older skater knew important people. You see, Eddie worked down at The Flight Deck, the local skateboard shop. He captained The Flight Deck's skateboard team, which Craig and Dane hoped to join. And, as captain, Eddie had a major say as to who joined the team.

"Okay, Grommet!" Eddie called Craig by his nickname, reminding me I still didn't know what it meant. "Let's get into the pool."

Every skater watched as Eddie and Craig dropped down into the empty concrete swimming pool. I did, too. The skate park was incredible! In addition to the pool, it had ramps, a halfpipe and tons of *street terrain*. It may have been the coolest place I had ever seen.

Eddie started by showing Craig a few moves inside the pool. To the delight of the crowd, Craig copied every one of them, only better. I leaned in closer to the action. It was awesome. After Craig finished his run inside the pool, the look on Eddie's face said it all. He was jealous. Grommet Pederson was stealing the show.

I wanted to watch other guys, though. So I went over to the halfpipe, or *vert* ramp. A halfpipe is like a big U. The flat bottom in the middle extends up on either side to a platform. The kid I saw, after dropping off one platform, was a blur. He sped atop the sides of the U, doing kick turns at each lip. *Would I ever be able to do that?*

Then I turned to study Hot Dog Armour. He

was in the process of *grinding* along several hand-rails. Grinding meant sliding one's board along the edge or top of an object. You did this on the axles of both trucks. The *trucks* connect the wheels to the board, or deck. Grinding looked fun but not easy to do.

Just when I thought I'd seen everything, I found Grommet Pederson atop the vert ramp. He gave me a wave before heading down and then up the other side. Once there, he flew through the air with one hand on his board. His other hand was on the edge of the ramp. Meanwhile, his feet were pointed to the sky with the skateboard stuck to them. Even more amazing was how he landed—on his board—heading the opposite way!

It was the most unbelievable thing I had ever seen. Not only did it take guts, but it also displayed great athletic talent. On seeing it, the skateboarders at the park burst into applause. I think I clapped the loudest. I wanted to learn how to do the exact same thing.

Craig and Dane were fearless. It didn't matter if they were on a ramp, a rail or a ledge. No challenge seemed too great. They performed tricks that defined modern-day skateboarding. The sport had become an artistic display of style, power and passion.

I quickly realized I had been wrong about these guys and the sport. Sure, some skaters looked and talked differently than the jocks I had known. They weren't the troublemakers I made them out to be, though. Craig and Dane were committed to their sport. The only difference was that they didn't focus on rules, positions, teammates, playbooks, strategy or winning. It seemed they gave a 100-percent effort just to do what they did well, really well. The rush they got when they mastered a trick was their reward.

That's why, when my turn to give it a shot came up, I was ready. I wanted to feel that rush. First, Dane gave me his helmet and pads. Then Craig held up his board. "I don't let just anyone use this board," he said. "But you've never skated before. I'd hate to see you eat it because you're riding on someone's crappy deck. This board won't do you wrong. You 'slam' it while riding this," he added, "and it's *your* fault."

"Thanks," I said, half grateful and half nervous.

"Just take it nice and slow today, rookie," said Dane. "No need to get all funky. Don't even try any tricks until you and the board are like one," he added. "And that's gonna take some time."

"Dane's right," said Craig. "But if you *feel it,* and you might *feel it,* try an ollie." Craig saw something in me that he saw in himself—the will to succeed. We had never spoken about how I approached challenges. But he knew I would rise to this one. Guys like us never backed down.

Craig turned to Dane. "My guess is Flyboy here's a natural. Either way, he isn't gonna be happy till he's a skater. Isn't that right, Flyboy?"

I smiled at Grommet Pedersen. I liked the Air

Force-sounding nickname he had assigned me. "Definitely," I added.

But before I headed off to become a skateboarder, I needed to know something. "Why do they call you Grommet?" I asked.

Craig laughed. "A grommet is a little-kid skater. I started skateboarding when I was 3, and some older guys started calling me that. It fit, and it stuck."

"Easier nickname to live up to than mine," I said.

"Not very cool, though," Craig said. "Flyboy, now that's cool."

"Yeah, but what do I say when people ask me how I got my nickname?"

Craig looked down at the board, then back at me. "Tell them you can fly. Who knows, if you're good enough, it might be true."

CHAPTER FIVE

BASIC TRAINING

With Craig looking over my shoulder, I carefully mounted the deck. At first, I didn't know what to do. Sure, I had been watching a lot lately. But now that I was actually on top of a skateboard, I was unsure of myself.

Once the board started to move beneath my feet, everything changed. I stopped thinking and just started to roll. A huge smile swept across my face. Something about being on top of that board made sense. I can't really explain it. It was a comfortable feeling—like I had just gotten home from a long trip.

I balanced myself, bent my knees, then started to sway back and forth to get a feel for the deck. After a deep breath, I was ready. So I pushed off with one foot, like I had seen other skaters do. The board shot forward with me on top. I nearly fell off. Then I slowly moved along the concrete. I could feel every bump and change in the slope, too.

I picked up some speed, kicking off the ground with a bit more force. *This is so cool*, I thought, as the wind hit me in the face. At top speed, the ride became softer, smoother. With both feet back on the board now, I began to make small turns. I'd move left, then right.

The grainy tape on Craig's board gave my feet—and my confidence—what they needed. I was ready to try something more challenging. But, I couldn't. I needed to learn the basics first.

Craig's instructions were simple, "Don't think. Just ride." I did just that as I toured the skate park. . . . atop a skateboard.

After watching for a few minutes, Craig started to coach me. He informed me that I was a goofy-footer. I skated with my right foot forward. A *switch stance* for me was left foot forward. Craig insisted I go back and forth between my regular stance and my switch stance.

Hot Dog chimed in, saying this would help me "become one with the board."

I followed the training course they outlined, practicing on the park's tamer terrain. I worked on dropping off curbs, switching feet and trying a few spins.

I fell quite a bit. After falling, I'd do a quick head-to-toe search for injuries. Once I'd determined nothing was broken, I'd hop back on. . . . only to fall again. That's the way it went for most of that day.

I kept at it. I knew that if I gave up, I'd never become a skater. I had too much determination to let that happen. Craig knew it. Before long, so did Dane and the rest of the kids at the skateboard park.

According to Craig, I would get better if I stuck to his advice. "Try not to get stuck on any one problem," he said. "You'll need to put in a lot of time on each new skill. But at every skate session, try and mix it up. That way, you'll develop a flow. When you start feeling frustrated by something, just move on to something else." He was right. It was easier to try a number of different things. My legs started to loosen up, and I began moving more gracefully.

Craig borrowed one of the many boards Eddie always brought with him to the park. He joined me and Dane after a while. Skating with them was awesome! Thanks to their advanced ability, I started to really make strides.

My progress that afternoon was well-noted. I heard shouts of appreciation from quite a few kids at the skate park. They liked that an "old man" of 14 was learning how to skate. Most of these kids had been skating since they were 7 or 8. I definitely had some catching up to do.

Although I was enjoying myself, this sport was frustrating. I don't think I'd fallen so much in my whole life! But I had to do more than just make an effort. I wanted to prove myself as a skater. I knew I'd have to get good fairly soon. If not, I'd be laughed out of the park, never to jam again.

In order to avoid this fate, Craig said I *had* to nail an ollie. I didn't have to make it perfect. I just had to pull one off. I remembered what I read on the plane ride over from Germany. Every other air trick is based on the ollie. Once it's learned, a skater can fly over any obstacle in his path. Only then could I manage other tricks and earn some "street cred."

I practiced hard for the next few hours. Rolling off the park's curbs, I got some air under me. Each time I did, I gained confidence. My feet and the board were operating as one. I listened closely as Craig played the role of trainer. "Put the ball of your back foot in the middle of the deck's tail." He was referring to the rear of the board. "And your goofy foot goes between the middle of the deck and the front truck."

I wobbled a bit as I moved my feet. I righted myself and got ready for what was next.

"Now, practice bending down," he added. "The goal is to become an extension of the board. Either that or the board becomes an extension of you."

"It's all very cosmic, dude," said Dane, who just then skated by.

I laughed at Dane, and then began making myself "small." I dropped the weight of my body down into my legs, then into my feet. I tried to put imaginary dents into the deck. Then I slammed my back foot on the kicktail. It slapped against the ground, while the front of the board popped up.

"Now, leap into the air," Craig said.

"What?"

"You heard me. As you slam the kicktail down, lift up like you're an airplane taking off. That shouldn't be hard for you, Flyboy."

It *was* hard, though, really hard. But I was determined to do it. So I got down to business. I pushed off and got up some speed. Boring holes into the board with my feet, I went into my crouch. With my goofy foot steering, I released my left knee from near my chest. Then, with my left foot, I stomped down on the tail of the board.

The smack it made against the pavement was loud. I heard it long after I had become airborne. And it echoed in my ears when I landed flat on my back. "Now what?" I asked Craig as a small stream of blood trickled down my shin.

"Once you're in the air, lift your knees up toward your chest," he said. "At the same time, rub your right foot along the board toward the nose. And remember, you're not just jumping up, you're jumping forward."

Whoa, I thought as I got to my feet. *All that just to start every other trick?* This was the hardest thing I'd ever tried to do! Which, of course, made me want to do it more.

I worked at it for nearly another hour. I was getting pretty close to pulling it off. I was also getting pretty tired. The sun was fading. I knew I should probably head home, but I just couldn't leave.

At this point, I was able to pop up into the air pretty well. I was also able to suck up my knees so they bumped against my chest. I just couldn't do both at the same time yet. I took a deep breath, closed my eyes and focused. I tried to visualize myself nailing an ollie. In my head, I pictured the trick in slow motion. I took note of what each part of my body did. When I opened my eyes, I was ready. "Okay," I said to Craig, "I can do this."

"I know you can," Craig smiled. "Now *do* it already!"

Once again, I pushed off, placed my feet correctly, crouched and popped. Then, while airborne, I jumped "ahead." As I flew upward and forward, the wind blew in my face. The shapes of the skate park became a blur. What an amazing feeling! As I came down, I realized my feet were still attached to the deck.

The lights of the skateboard park came on the moment I touched down. I had nailed the perfect ollie! I lifted my hand up in the air and pumped my fist. I couldn't have been more fired up.

"Nice air!" shouted Hot Dog.

I flashed the biggest smile I could. In this moment, I realized something about myself: I was addicted to skateboarding.

"Well, well, well, just as I thought," said Craig. "Flyboy can skate!"

Less than a half hour later, I ran through the front door of our house. I couldn't wait to tell my parents what happened. It didn't even dawn on me that I was late for dinner.

"Mom, Dad, guess what?" I shouted as I made my way toward the kitchen. Turning the corner to see them already eating, I swallowed hard.

"Where have you been, Airman?" My father's voice had a way of carrying. I stopped in my tracks. *Uh-oh*, I thought to myself. Tardiness was not tolerated in Colonel Hardin's world, no matter what the reason. "Well?" he asked.

My eyes were locked on the floor. "I was at the skateboard park with a couple of guys from school," I answered. "I'm sorry, but I was having so much fun I lost track of time." I couldn't help but smile, thinking about the ollie I had landed only minutes before.

Mom smiled, too. I could tell she was happy I was settling in, making friends and feeling good.

Dad didn't smile, though. "You know how I feel about being late," he said. His eyes had a way of piercing a hole through you.

"I know," I said.

"If you knew, then why were you late?" he asked, still glaring at me.

"I don't know," I said, looking in his eyes.

"You know, and you don't know," he said. "Now, what am I to make of that, Airman?"

I remained silent.

Dad knew I had no answer. So he picked up right where he left off. "I don't want you hanging around with a bunch of skateboarders. And not only because they kept you from being at the dinner table on time."

"What do you mean?" I asked. "I'll make sure to wear my watch down to the skate park." I looked over at Mom. "I won't be late again. I . . ."

Dad cut me off. "Those are not the kind of kids I want you spending your time with, Toby."

His comment bothered me. "Exactly what kind of kids *are* they?" I asked.

"Watch your tone," he said, stopping in mid-bite to point his fork at me.

"Sorry," I said, looking down at my plate.

"They're the kind of kids who don't join in," my dad said. He sounded like he had written the book on skateboarders.

Still, I knew I *had* to argue my point. Especially because I had thought the same thing. I had felt the same way my father had, until I met Craig and Dane. They deserved to have someone defend them, as any good soldier should do. Besides, I had fallen in love with skateboarding. There was no turning back now.

"Dad," I began. "I think . . ."

He interrupted me. "I don't want to see you end up wasting your life."

My mind was racing. *Wasting my life?* How

could afternoons at the skateboard park turn into me wasting my life? He didn't think I was wasting my life playing soccer. Why was soccer worthy and skateboarding not? Was it because of the way skaters dressed? Was it because of some of the slang they used? Although these questions flooded my brain, I tried to stay calm.

I continued thinking before I spoke. Sure, I knew skateboarding would never have a place alongside baseball in Dad's mind. That was okay with me. Soccer hadn't either. But I was surprised when he dumped on it so strongly. I finished chewing a piece of pot roast and spoke softly. "How do you figure I'll end up wasting my life?"

My mom prepared for the worst. But my question was a reasonable one, and my need for an answer was genuine.

"Those kids are into a lifestyle that's all about rebellion, Toby. They go against the grain and they cause trouble," my dad said. "They end up not making a difference in the world. They're not taken seriously by anyone. You, Airman, *are* going to make a difference." And with that, he stuck a large helping of food into his mouth.

With Dad chewing, I had my chance to say something. "Dad, I have every intention of making something of myself. I hope you know that about me by now. I'm not a troublemaker," I said. "But I really love skateboarding. I mean, in one day, I was doing stuff I didn't think was possible. I'd like to see what I can do with this sport."

Mom's smile indicated I had handled that well. I didn't raise my voice, I didn't get mad. I simply challenged my father in a way that made sense. She turned to him. "I think the fact that Toby has found something that interests him is very important."

Dad swallowed and stared at Mom.

"It sure is!" I said. "I'm really into skateboarding—the sport, that is, not the people who do it."

I knew I was stretching the truth a bit. I'm sure my mom knew it, too. I liked Craig and Dane almost as much as I liked skateboarding.

"Come on, Dad. Please, just let me try it out for a while," I continued.

My dad put down his fork and folded his hands under his chin. Then he looked up at me and spoke. "I don't think it's a good idea, Toby." He spoke calmly. "Just keep up your training and your schoolwork. Soccer season will be here sooner than you think." This comment put an end to the conversation.

The house was silent the rest of the night.

CHAPTER SIX

THE NEW WORLD

I was going to have to skate without my father knowing. This would be hard. I had never kept anything from him before, much less disobeyed an order. But he hadn't left me a choice. Skateboarding was something I just *had* to do.

Deep down, I knew Dad wanted me to be happy. He also wanted to protect me. I understood his concerns, and I respected them. Dad didn't want me to waste my life or rebel. I wasn't planning on doing either. I just wanted to get on a skateboard and jam. How could he have a problem with that?

First things first, though. I needed a deck. Luckily, I had saved up enough money from work. So I headed over to The Flight Deck to buy my first board. Craig and Dane offered to help me pick it out. As a result, there were no shortages of opinion. "Choose a deck designed for the kind of riding you're going to do," said Craig. "Street skating, vert skating or both."

"Nah, just pick the deck you feel the most spiritually connected to," said Hot Dog. "Either that, or the one with the coolest graphics."

We were in the store, surrounded by more skateboarding gear than I'd ever seen. I was starting to realize how complicated this process was.

Eddie Rios, recently promoted manager, brought out several decks for me to look at. Dane went off to watch a skateboard video playing on the shop's television. Craig stayed with me and continued talking. "Flyboy, you're gonna be doing a lot of street skating if you hang with us. That means doing lip tricks and grinds on rails and ledges. So you need a deck that's not too wide."

I nodded. It made sense. A thinner deck would be much easier to flip.

"But, you'll be skating ramps, too, plus the pool over at the park," added Craig. "So you'll need a deck with a bit more width. A wider board will give you more of a surface to land on."

I understood this as well. In the pool or on a ramp, balance is the key. A wider deck would be easier to control.

Craig continued. "You need a deck around 8 inches wide," he said. "Like mine."

Eddie approached us after grabbing a board from the back room. He half-jokingly pushed Craig back a few feet. "Back up, Grommet! You don't work here, remember? I do. Here, Flyboy. Try this one." Eddie handed me a jet-black deck. "It's 8 inches across."

I placed it on the ground and stood on it.

"Make sure the nose and tail aren't too steep," said Craig.

Eddie shot Craig a dirty look. "Hey, who's the salesman here?" Eddie said sharply.

"You are," said Craig. "But since you weren't doing it, I figured I better help educate your customer."

"I don't need your help, Grommet," said Eddie. "I'll get your rookie the right board."

At that, Craig left to join Dane on the other side of the store. I felt uncomfortable, being in the middle of a confrontation between Craig and Eddie. It seemed like whenever these two were together, there was tension.

"Guy thinks he's hot stuff," Eddie said to me as Craig walked away. "I showed that kid everything I know. Now that he's gotten pretty good he thinks he's better than me." Eddie shook his head, changing the subject. "Anyway, what do you think of this deck?"

I moved my feet up and down the black piece of wood. It was wide enough—but not so wide I'd have trouble flipping it. "I like it, but do you have the same one in blue?" I asked Eddie.

"You'd rather have blue than black?" he asked. "You know, black is *the* color this year."

"Yeah, but with a name like Flyboy, I ought to

have a blue deck."

Eddie gave me a nasty look. "I might have one in the back." He disappeared through a door behind the counter.

Craig and Dane came back over. "Now you need the right trucks and wheels," Craig said. I followed Craig around the store. I quickly learned that, like decks, trucks come in different sizes.

"When choosing trucks, make sure they're almost as wide as your deck," said Craig. "If they're too thin, you'll have a wobbly ride. If they're too wide, your deck won't respond during turns."

We found a pair of *mids,* ideal for all-around skating. Then, we moved on to wheels and bearings. Just then, Eddie came out of the back room with the blue deck. "You need trucks, Flyboy," he said. "Here's a pair of high ones."

"I already picked out a pair, mids, though."

Eddie made a face at Craig, before disappearing into the storeroom again.

"Forget him," said Craig. "He thinks he's the only one who knows anything about skateboarding. Half the kids at the park know more than Eddie."

"I know I do," said Hot Dog. He was holding up a pair of wheels for me to check out. They were small, but not too small, and hard to the touch. "These will give you a light setup and keep you lower to the ground. They're ideal for tricks."

"Great wheels," Craig said, handing me the set

Dane picked out. "Having the right wheels doesn't mean squat if you don't have decent bearings, though. Use these." He handed me a set of bearings. "They're not too expensive to replace if you abuse them, which you will."

A moment later Eddie returned, carrying a helmet, pads, grip tape, nuts and bolts. He dropped everything on the counter with a crash. "Ready to pay?" he asked, as he adjusted the rubber band on his ponytail.

"Yup," I said.

"You're gonna assemble the board for him at no extra cost, right, Eddie?" asked Craig. "It says so on the sign." Craig pointed to a sign above the register.

Eddie glared at Craig without speaking. Hot Dog let out a laugh. Just then, the skateboard video, with its loud music, came to a stop. As a result, The Flight Deck got deathly quiet.

"I'll have time tomorrow," Eddie said slowly. He sounded like he was making it up as he went along. He looked over at Craig. "I have to drive up to Melbourne tonight. I'm checking out this skater who's hoping to make The Flight Deck team. I hear he can rip."

Craig's eyes narrowed. I figured out immediately what was going on. Eddie felt threatened by Grommet's progress. That's why he was mentioning a team prospect in Melbourne, a town up the coast.

He was trying to mess with Craig's head. Craig knew Eddie had final say regarding who made The Flight Deck team. Mentioning someone who wasn't even a local was a real slap in the face.

"Tomorrow's fine," said Craig on my behalf. He motioned to Dane and me to follow him out of the store. We did silently. Once outside, we all started talking at once.

"Melbourne!" said Dane, angrily. "He's gonna look at some guy who's not even a local! That punk shouldn't even be able to try out."

"You got that right," said Craig. "Sebastian's skateboard team should be made up of locals."

So these guys did believe in the locals only beach-town philosophy. I couldn't help but wonder if they considered *me* a local. I lived in town now, but I *was* an outsider, no question. Not that it really mattered. I had no shot at making The Flight Deck squad anyway. I had barely managed my first ollie the day before.

"That really stinks," I said out loud. I felt bad for my new friends. I understood why they were upset. Eddie Rios could purposely leave Craig off the team. That way, he wouldn't be shown up by a younger, more talented skater. If Craig skated for The Flight Deck, he would shine like a star. Eddie knew this. Putting some kid from 20 miles up the road on the team just wasn't fair.

"Let's slow down, guys," Craig said, trying to

ease our worries. "No need to start buggin' out. It won't do Eddie any good to leave me off the team. He knows I can help him get where he's dying to go."

"Where's that?" I asked.

"Under the spotlight," said Craig.

I nodded my head and smiled. I respected Craig's calm and cool confidence.

"What about me?" asked Hot Dog, still uncertain.

"You know I don't go anywhere without my boy," said Craig. "Eddie would be a fool not to take you, too. You rip!" Craig looked over at me. "Plus, if Flyboy learns fast, Eddie might have to take all three of us!"

I shouldn't have even been in the conversation. I wasn't anywhere near their league as a skateboarder. Still, it was nice to know Craig thought I had what it took. It was also great knowing these were my friends, despite what my father thought.

"When does Eddie choose the roster?" I asked.

"He makes his final decision over the winter," said Dane. "That gives you about three months to learn how to skate, Flyboy. The team starts competing in amateur contests in the spring."

"If you make the team, who do you skate against?" I asked.

"You skate against other teams from other towns, sponsored by other stores," said Craig. "You know, there was a time when all the local shops had killer teams. But now, skateboarding has gotten too big. The corner store has a hard time competing for talent. The big companies have the best teams now."

I was confused, figuring most of this stuff out on the fly. "Let me get this straight," I said. "Basically, skaters sign on with different skateboard companies, or local stores like The Flight Deck. Then the skaters compete as a team against other skaters who are representing other companies? Is that right?"

"Exactly," Craig said.

"Why not just enter the contests on your own?" I asked.

"Because of guys like Bud LaCross, who owns The Flight Deck," Dane said. "Bud will pay for us to travel and give us free gear. It's a righteous deal."

"What does The Flight Deck get out of it?" I asked.

"Well, if we win, the Flight Deck gets a ton of publicity," said Dane.

"Most of the major skateboard companies send representatives to the local contests," Craig added. "They're looking for new talent who can represent their boards, clothes and other skate gear. If you're good enough, one of the big companies will sign you." Following this comment, Craig and Dane bumped knuckles.

My head was spinning. Competitive skateboarding was much more organized than I had thought. Somewhere between the Z Boys and the X-Games, the sport had somehow grown up. It seemed very professional. Apparently, the major skateboard brands and clothing companies were calling the shots.

"Two of Flight Deck's best skaters were recently picked up by a major sponsor. Eddie got left behind, and now he's mad," said Craig.

"That's why there are a few spots open this year," said Dane, his eyes sparkling.

Craig beamed. "The quickest way to turn pro is to skate for The Flight Deck. Compete in some local contests and then get signed by one of the big boys."

"Is that what you want to do, turn pro?" I asked.

"Are you kidding? Make money skateboarding! What could be better than that?"

That night, I read more about competitive skateboarding online. I found out this new corporate skateboarding world bothered a lot of the skateboard pioneers. They often complained that the best skaters today had sold out to sponsorship. They had forgotten why they started skating in the first place. I saw their point. Skating because it was fun had taken a backseat to making a living at it. This definitely changed the beauty of the sport.

I picked up my board from Eddie after school the next day. He asked whether I was heading over to the skate park to meet Craig. When I told him yes, he said he'd be over in a little while. This made me wonder if Eddie had something important to tell Craig. Like . . . the kid from Melbourne was so good that Craig needn't bother trying out.

At the park, I met up with Grommet and Hot Dog. They were already carving it up big time in the pool. I told Craig I thought Eddie wanted to see him. Then I headed over to the curbs and rails to practice my ollies and grinds.

Before long, Eddie arrived. I stopped what I was doing to watch as he approached the pool. "Hey, Grommet!" he called. "I want to talk to you."

From a distance, I watched the two of them. After about 15 minutes, Craig and Eddie embraced in a brief hug. Eddie then turned and made his way back to his car. I jogged over to Craig as Hot Dog climbed out of the bowl. "What did Eddie want?" I asked.

Craig looked uncomfortable, like he had just seen a ghost. "Nothing," he said. "It's all good. He told me that the guy in Melbourne was a poser. Eddie knows what he has to do. The only way he's ever going to make it is if The Flight Deck team is awesome. The only way that's going to happen is if I'm on it. He's got to put me on the team."

"Did he say anything about me?" asked Dane.

An awkward look came over Craig's face. "No, he didn't. But he knows where I stand when it comes to that."

We all stared across the park at Eddie as he drove away. What followed was a strange silence.

Although it appeared that Craig's explanation was enough for Dane, I couldn't help but worry. Craig was a much better skateboarder than Hot Dog. Anyone could see that. I wondered: *What if an opportunity came his way that didn't include Hot Dog? Would he take it?*

Everything I knew about Craig said his answer would be "no." I was sure that Dane and Craig would both be skating for The Flight Deck. And I'd be right there cheering them on.

CHAPTER SEVEN

PERMISSION TO SKATE, SIR

My dad wasn't happy come mid-October. That's when I told him I wanted to blow off winter soccer camp. Of course, I didn't tell him I had been busy skateboarding the past few months. I also failed to mention I was no longer interested in soccer. Instead, I told him I was too busy with schoolwork and at Dex's.

It was a giant lie.

My transition from Germany to Florida had actually been smoother than I had expected. Sure, I was disappointed about not being able to play soccer. But it had all turned out okay. Within a few weeks, I had discovered skateboarding, found some great friends and was happy. Things were great, except for one thing. I couldn't stand lying to my father. I wanted to confess, but I was scared he'd take skateboarding away from me.

Over time, I figured out what Dad had against skateboarding. The sport was not like all the others I had played. That was part of the reason why I liked it so much! Before I started skating, sports for me meant rules, coaches and discipline. Skateboarding, on the other hand, had none of that. It was all about individual expression, going at your own pace, answering to no one. *Freedom!* The only limits were those you put on yourself.

A sport without rules or apparent discipline made Dad's skin crawl. As did the shaggy haircuts and baggy pants that often went along with it.

Regardless of how he felt, I didn't think I could keep lying much longer. After living in Florida for a couple of months, I was a pretty good skater. I considered the sport my absolute favorite. Not being able to share that with my dad was tearing me apart. One way or another, I needed him to know about my secret.

It turned out that Dad was already on to me. He had taken off early from work one day, without me or Mom knowing. He stood outside his car, on a hill a half-mile away. Through his high-powered binoculars, he watched me skate. Not knowing he was there, I spent the afternoon practicing the *kickflip*. According to Craig, landing a kickflip would help fine-tune a smoother style.

The kickflip began, as most other stunts, with an ollie. But then it got hard. Under Craig's watchful eye, I was to start from my regular ollie stance. As before, I was to move my back foot to the tail of the board. I was to pop down really hard in order to catch some good air. As the nose pointed skyward, I was to slide my front foot forward. Only, this time, I would flick my front foot off the tip of the nose. This would cause the board to spin. If I did it right, it would flip a full 360 degrees.

Now, if I made it that far, all that was left was the *catch*. In the end, the goal was to land cleanly, absorb the shock and skate away.

I fell more times than I'd care to remember practicing. So did a lot of kids at the park. Most of them, though, were attempting simpler maneuvers than a kickflip. But I knew if I wanted to push the envelope, I had to go further. Eating gravel was my motivation. As Craig repeated to me again and again, I was not an average beginner. For some reason, skateboarding and Toby Hardin clicked.

A few hours after finally landing a kickflip, I headed home for dinner. Ever since that first time, I made sure never to be late again. I didn't want to draw unwanted heat from my father.

"Frustrating, isn't it?" Dad asked, a few minutes after we had sat down.

"What is?" I asked, diving into a piece of Mom's fried chicken.

"Trying to master something that doesn't seem possible," my father said.

I glanced up at him with a puzzled look.

He gazed at me stone-faced before saying, "I saw you at the skate park today."

I coughed, nearly choking. I didn't know what to say, so I waited for Dad to speak. Finally, he did. "Care to explain yourself?"

I could see myself being grounded for the rest of my life. "You saw me skate?" I asked.

"Yes, I did," he said.

"Dad, I . . ."

My father cut me off, although his voice was strangely calm. "I'm not sure if skipping soccer camp will one day prove to be a mistake. I can't see the future, Toby. But what I saw you doing today registered with me on a number of levels."

What was that? What did he just say? I couldn't believe what I was hearing. "Huh?" was all I could come up with.

"Listen to me, Toby," he said, leaning forward in his chair. "You were wrong to disobey me. Lying to me for the past few months was dishonorable. It was cowardly."

"I know, sir," I said. "I'm sorry." I looked down at my plate.

He stood up and began walking around the table. "Toby, sometimes a commanding officer will give an order that doesn't make sense. A good soldier has to be willing to question that order. If he can't carry it out, he has a duty to say so." His voice became louder.

"But it is *NEVER* acceptable to simply not follow it!"

"Dad, I tried, but you didn't understand how I …"

He interrupted me again. "Your mother and I have been talking a lot about you lately. We think you're a great kid, Toby." He paused. "And I may have done you a disservice," he said. "I should have trusted you to handle the new world you're a part of. I apologize for that."

"Apology accepted," I said. "And I apologize for lying. It's been killing me every day, Dad, honest."

"Apology accepted, Airman." The colonel smiled slightly. "Well, I'm retired, and I guess I'm softening a bit. So, I'm not grounding you for lying to me."

I looked down at my plate once again. "Thank you, sir."

Dad's voice brightened a bit. "Anything worth-while takes effort, Toby. I saw you refusing to quit today. I admire that. I was very proud watching you try to land that trick." He looked over at my mother. "He is really something on that skateboard." Then he looked back at me. "You really are, Toby."

I smiled.

"To be honest, I saw everyone else at the park doing the same thing. They were all striving for excellence," Dad added. "It reminded me of basic training back at Lackland—without the instructor shouting, of course."

"So," I said cautiously, "do I have your permission to skate?"

"On three conditions," my dad said.

"What are they?" I asked.

"One, you keep working at Dex's," he said. "You do not quit your job just so you can skateboard. Understand?"

"Yes sir," I said.

"Two, if I find out that these boys are like I suspected, you're done. Is that clear?"

"Yes, sir," I responded again, this time with more emphasis.

"And, three, you have to invite your old man down there once in a while. I want to watch you skate— and not through binoculars."

"Okay," I said, smiling broadly. "You got a deal." I extended my hand, and we shook.

Dad returned to his seat and his fried chicken. "That's all, Airman."

CHAPTER EIGHT

THE DEAL

Over the next several months, I skated nearly every day. A giant weight had been lifted off of my shoulders when my secret was exposed. I was now able to skate and then come home and tell my parents all about it. Their support, as much as anything else, made me a more complete skater. After all, Colonel Hardin thought I had talent. Dad wasn't known for giving out unnecessary compliments. If he said you were good at something, chances are you were.

During the next few months, Dad became my biggest fan. He came down to the park at least once a week. He'd even watch skateboard videos with me at home sometimes. Once, I caught him walking into the bathroom with one of my skateboarding magazines!

In the meantime, I had taken my hobby to another level. Aside from school, I was almost always skating with Craig and Dane at the park. I did adopt their wardrobe, but I just couldn't let my hair grow. The guys kidded me constantly about it. They'd say my buzz cut just wasn't right for the skateboard scene. I disagreed with them and planned on keeping my hair "high and tight," as my dad described it.

I always told Craig the same thing. "I love skateboarding, Grommet. But that doesn't mean I want a greasy head of hair like yours. Besides," I reminded him, "I wouldn't be Flyboy if I didn't have a military cut."

The three of us had been inseparable since September. Nothing changed throughout the rest of the fall. We spent every minute we could skating together. We were really close, especially Craig and I. He was like the brother I never had.

During this time, I was making daily improvements on a skateboard. By early December, I was able to hang with Hot Dog at the park. Surprisingly to everyone except Craig, I was becoming one of the better skaters in town. I was especially good at vert skating stunts.

Everything was going great until winter arrived. That's when things began to change between the three of us. Craig was pulling further away from the rest of the skaters in Sebastian. This was probably why he suddenly stopped hanging out with us.

What Dane and I didn't know was that Craig and Eddie had struck a deal. It was hard to believe, but true. It left Hot Dog and me on the outside looking in.

From that point on, Craig was always somewhere else. And he always had an excuse as to why he couldn't hang out. Initially, I took Craig's word for it, until I started to notice something. Whenever he *was* at the park, Eddie was, too. And when Craig was absent, Eddie was nowhere to be found.

Even though I tried, I couldn't ignore the signs. Something was going on. I later found out exactly what it was. Eddie Rios was getting paranoid. He was worried about competing against Craig Pederson. He knew that Grommet would be the star of The Flight Deck team. All eyes would be on Craig, not him. He was scared that some big company would give Craig a better deal and that he would be left behind.

Eddie figured he could convince a company that he and Craig were a team—that they couldn't sign Craig without signing him, too. Then Eddie's career would soar as high as Craig's.

The first part of their deal involved Craig cutting ties with Dane and me. Eddie was in Craig's ear every day. "I talk to these sponsors all the time, Grommet. I know how it works. You don't."

Eddie would plead with Craig. "If you hang out with amateurs, the big companies will ignore you. They'll come to the local event and watch you skate. But when they see you with Hot Dog and Flyboy, they'll think you're small-time.

"Stick with me, and we'll get to the top. …

together."

It wasn't true, but Craig bought into it. "All right, Eddie, you've got a deal. You and me, we're a team."

Not having my friend around hurt. I knew deep down that Craig didn't *want* to abandon us. Eddie, the 18-year-old with all the connections, had convinced him he *needed* to.

Even though Craig wasn't around, Dane and I skated. We'd still call Craig and tell him to meet us at the park. Usually, he didn't show up. He'd tell us the next day at school that he was sorry. Most of the time, though, he avoided us altogether.

When we *did* see him long enough to talk, he never explained what was happening. He'd mumble something about some odd job he had to do. And that's about all he'd say. It was frustrating, and it made us sad. Our best friend had decided that he was done with us. Just like that.

I could tell Craig wasn't comfortable with his decision, though. He seemed to be wrestling with it. Dane and I both noticed how it didn't look like he enjoyed blowing us off. Craig looked like he wished he could come with us. It was as if he were a puppet, unable to control his own actions. Dane and I suspected that Eddie was the puppeteer, pulling the strings behind the scenes.

I had lost my best friend. … again. Only this time, I couldn't blame it on my dad.

Everything came to a head on a late January afternoon at the skateboard park. The place was packed. Hot Dog and I were taking a break from a hard session on the halfpipe. We chugged a couple of sports drinks to replenish the fluids our bodies had lost.

That was when Craig arrived. We knew something was wrong the minute we saw him. Stumbling out of Eddie's car, he came over. He appeared to wobble a bit as he approached us.

"Hey, Grommet!" called Hot Dog, as Craig approached. "Where've you been? You should have seen Flyboy today. Dude, he was sick!"

I blushed. It *had* been a great afternoon for me. I had been doing *180 ollies* and *fakie ollie grabs* all day on the halfpipe.

The second trick was a new one for me. It involved riding backward—*fakie*—up the ramp. At the top of the incline, I'd smack my back wheel on the coping. That's the metal piping along the top edge of the ramp. The sound it made would echo across the park, turning all heads my way. Then I'd suck my legs up into my chest and grab my board with my right hand. I'd float down before letting go, trying to land in the transition. That's the part of the halfpipe that is neither horizontal nor vertical.

"Sorry I missed it," Craig said. It was his standard response, which was getting old. This time he had trouble getting the words out. He was slurring them. When the wind changed direction, a breeze came at us from behind his back. We both got a whiff.

"Dude," said Dane, "you reek."

"Yeah, Craig," I said. "You smell like you've been drinking." My parents would have a drink sometimes, so I knew what booze smelled like. It was strong and sour.

"I had a couple of beers," he said.

"What for?" I asked.

"To celebrate," he replied, then hiccupped loudly.

"Celebrate what?" asked Dane.

"Making the Javelina skateboard team," said Eddie, just then walking up behind Craig. He smelled even worse.

We didn't speak, probably because, at that moment, we *couldn't* speak. Dane and I were in shock. Did he say that he and Craig made the Javelina skateboard team? *How did that happen?* we wondered.

Everybody at the park knew all about Javelina. The Javelina [pronounced ha-ve-LEE-na] Skateboard Company was a new firm out of Tucson, Arizona. Javelina made handcrafted, hardwood skateboards. Its logo was an angry, wild and hairy southwestern pig on a skateboard. And its gear was in demand. Apparently, so was Craig.

"What about The Flight Deck?" Finally able to speak, Dane asked the question that was on both our minds.

"We both made Javelina's team," said Eddie. "So neither of us will be skating for Flight Deck. In fact, I just came from there. I told Bud that I quit. If we want to go pro someday, we have to start training full time. Isn't that right, Grommet?"

"Yup," said Craig, who seemed to be having a hard time just standing up.

"So, you're leaving me behind after all," said Dane.

"Hot Dog," said Craig, still slurring. "I'd be crazy not to do this."

"How'd they come to pick you?" I asked.

Pointing a shaky finger at me, Eddie interrupted. "Last weekend, Craig and I competed in the Tampa Am."

Dane and I just looked at each other. The Tampa Am was one of the biggest amateur skateboard events in the country. How did Craig and Eddie get into that tournament?

"Man, we were rad!" said Eddie. "We had reps from Dead Horse, Hard and Fast Skateboards, and Javelina checking us out. Then, today, we get a call from a dude at Javelina. He says he wants the two of us to represent his company. So, starting next week, we skate as Hogs."

He and Craig began to laugh.

"Both of you, huh?" I asked. "You've got a good grip on Craig's coattails, don't you, Eddie?

You're gonna ride him all the way to the top, huh?"

"Shut your mouth, Flyboy!" said Eddie. "I was carvin' it up on a board long before you ever got here."

I looked over at Craig, "Do you really need this guy to get where you're going, Craig? Is this really worth it? Can't you see what he's doing?"

Craig didn't respond. He just looked down at his feet.

"Whatever, Flyboy," Eddie shrugged. "Craig wants to be a pro. Hanging out with you two dorks at the skate park isn't gonna make that happen. If you were his real friends, you'd be happy for him and shut up." Eddie took a large sip from a beer can he was holding.

I looked over at Craig again. His gaze was still fixed on the ground. Apparently, he didn't have the guts to look Dane and me in the eye. It wasn't right. We knew the only reason Eddie was on the Javelina team was because of Craig. This made it harder to understand why Craig was giving Eddie so much respect. I thought back to the day I bought my board at The Flight Deck. Craig made Eddie look like a poser. Why this sudden change?

Then again, it wasn't really sudden. This had been coming on ever since Eddie checked out that skater in Melbourne. The conversation that followed at the skate park was when this thing really started. Eddie must have given Craig a choice. He could either do it Eddie's way or be left off The Flight Deck team.

Looking at that kid in Melbourne was Eddie's message to Craig. It said: "You're not the only skater out there, Grommet."

I continued to press Craig. "Since when do you drink?" I asked. I knew I sounded like my father, but I didn't care. Craig was my friend. I didn't want him to become one of *those* kids my father associated skateboarding with. As a good soldier, and a good friend, it was my duty to confront him.

"First time," said Craig. "We were celebrating."

"Uh huh," I said, waiting for Craig to explain. I wanted to know why he went to the Tampa Am. Why he didn't invite us to go along. Why he wasn't interested in skating with us anymore. And why he felt the need to drink beer with a guy like Eddie Rios.

"I'm outta here," said Dane, shooting both Craig and Eddie a deadly look. "You coming, Flyboy?"

"Yea," I answered. "It stinks around here."

We took off. As we headed home, I listened to Dane. He talked about all the great times he and Craig had skateboarding. Then, he ripped into him. But Hot Dog saved his worst insults for Eddie. He finally said, "You know, Eddie isn't even from Sebastian. He's from Connecticut. That loser moved here when he was 15. He isn't one of us."

It suddenly got quiet.

"I gotta get home," he said, turning to me. "See ya tomorrow, dude."

"Yea," I responded. "See you tomorrow."

I rubbed my hand across the peach fuzz atop my head. I wondered: Did Hot Dog feel the same way about me? When it came down to it, was I just an outsider? *And would I always be one?*

CHAPTER NINE

THE OUTSIDER

When I got home, Mom told me dinner wouldn't be ready for another 20 minutes. That was a good thing, because I felt kind of sick. I went up to my room and fell onto my bed. After a deep breath, my stomach settled.

I thought about Hot Dog. He felt betrayed by Craig—and rightly so. They had been best friends since they were in kindergarten! Now Craig wouldn't give him the time of day. I couldn't imagine how deeply that hurt him.

I grabbed my skateboard from the floor. I held it upside down on my chest and spun the wheels. As I did, I stared at the ceiling, trying to make sense of it all.

I knew Javelina was a huge step forward in Craig's skateboarding career. Skating as a Hog would give him more exposure. I appreciated Craig's skills and was proud that he had been chosen. I related to his desire to be the best he could be. And I wouldn't have stood in his way if he had told me about Javelina. But he tried out behind my back.

Personally, I wasn't interested in being sponsored, or being discovered. Craig knew that. We had spoken about it before. As a 14-year-old, I was stoked to jam down at the park. Plus, I would never turn my back on my friends like he did. For me, skateboarding was as much about them as it was about the ride. Until recently, I thought Craig and I shared this feeling.

That didn't mean I didn't take my skateboarding seriously. Skateboarding appealed to my competitive nature—just differently than traditional sports did. I pushed myself to the limit to be the best I could be. I competed hard. … against myself.

For now, doing cool tricks on top of a skateboard was all I wanted. I loved doing it more than anything else simply because it felt right. This sport was an extension of *me*. Through skateboarding and my skateboarding friends, I was able to express myself like never before.

Everything seemed to come naturally to me as well. I had always been a thrill-seeking, hard-charging son of an Air Force colonel. The fact that I loved flying through the air on a board was no surprise. Skateboarding was the perfect match for what I planned on doing with my life, too. After college, I would follow in my father's footsteps and join the Air Force.

Now, I didn't want to command people like Dad did. I wanted to be in the cockpit myself. I would treat flying exactly as I had skateboarding. I would give everything I had to be the best I could be. That's why I wanted to make The Flight Deck team. Not to become a pro, but to continue to improve. And to skate alongside my friends.

In thinking about my dreams, my mind drifted back to Craig. He and I clicked because we shared the same outlook on life. What happened to him that changed all that? As I stared at the ceiling, I decided I had to confront Craig. I needed to ask him why he abandoned Dane and me. I couldn't just let this go. Like my dad taught me, if you want the answer, you ask the question.

I saw Grommet in the hallway before homeroom the next day. He was on his way to his locker. I made my way over to him.

He didn't look so good. "Man, you look like crap," I said.

"Thanks," he said, forcing a grin. "Woke up with a wicked headache." He rubbed his eyes. "I'll be okay."

Our eyes met. I asked him the million-dollar question. "So, do you want to tell me what's going on with you, Craig?"

"What's to tell?" he answered.

"Why'd you stop hanging out with us?" I asked. After the words came out of my mouth, I realized they sounded desperate. That was not what I had intended. It wasn't as if I couldn't get along without Craig Pedersen. That was absurd. My face changed, and I tried to correct myself. "I mean, Dane and I want to skate and hang out with you. You're never around, dude."

"Things have changed, you know," Craig said.

"What does that mean?" I asked.

"I mean, my skateboard career—it's taking off, Flyboy," he said.

"What career?" I asked. "You're 14."

"So?" he responded. "Tony Hawk turned pro at 14."

"Good for Tony Hawk," I said, then paused. "What's your rush?" I asked.

"I have my reasons," he said.

"Are they good enough to justify kissing Eddie Rios' butt?" I thought this question was a loaded one. But Craig responded like he expected it.

"To me they are," he said.

"What about skating for the fun of it?" I asked. "All that stuff you told me when I first met you. Was that just a bunch of crap?"

"I still love to skate," he said.

"You do?" I asked sarcastically.

Craig was quiet for a moment. The conversation could not have been more awkward. Finally, he spoke. "Look," he said, "Eddie knows the right people. I did what had to be done for my career. Why can't you respect that?"

I started to talk a little bit faster. "You're good, Craig. You don't need Eddie to make it to the top. You'll make it with Dane and me cheering you on. But that doesn't mean anything to you."

Craig didn't respond.

"Whatever," I said, backing off for the moment. "So, are we ever going to skate together again?"

"I don't know," he said. "I'll be working out with Javelina's Florida team."

"Yeah, I understand," I said. And I did, at least the part about him needing to train with his team. "Even though you kicked me to the curb, I'll be rooting for you, Craig. Hot Dog will be, too."

"Thanks," he said. I could have sworn he had tears in his eyes. He then blurted out, "We're still tight, you know?"

I gave him a confused look. I hadn't talked to Craig for this long in two months. *Still tight?* He hadn't shown up at the park the last 10 times I invited him. "Still tight?" I muttered. "I'll cheer for you, but I'm not gonna pretend we're still tight. We're not tight, Craig. I wish that were true, but it isn't. You need to face reality—you dropped Dane and me. We don't see you. We don't hear from you. And we don't know you."

Craig became defensive. "I saw you yesterday

at the park. Don't be so dramatic, Flyboy."

"You were drunk at the park. You could barely walk over to us. Like I said, I don't know you any more."

An angry look came over his face. "Like I told you, yesterday was the first time I ever drank!"

"So, does that mean you're not going to do it again?" I asked. "Are you suddenly going to start calling me and Dane again? Or is that against the rules?" I raised my voice. "Eddie told you to stop seeing us, so you did! Eddie tells you to start drinking, and you do!"

Craig was yelling now, too. "Eddie's a fool! I do what I want to do! The beers are just part of the scene, Flyboy. Nobody tells me what to do! Who are you to judge me, soldier boy?" He stuck a finger in my chest. "You're not one of us. You never were. So what could you possibly understand? Besides, what do you know about skateboarding other than what *I've* taught you?"

He turned his back to me and started on down the hall.

I stood there for a moment, feeling sorry for myself. After hearing Dane and now Craig, I wondered. *Was* I still the shubee, the outsider, the kid who didn't belong?

Then, I got angry. After all, this wasn't about me. This was about Craig. "Who'd you say the fool was again?" I called after him. "Why don't you try looking in the mirror?"

I know he heard me, but he just kept on walking.

CHAPTER TEN

AIMING HIGHER

With Eddie gone, it was up to Bud La Cross to choose Flight Deck's roster. Bud had left the task to Eddie for the past few years. As a result, he wasn't up to speed on the local talent. So he had some scouting to do.

Bud was committed to picking the best skaters. That's because he wanted his logo displayed during the trophy presentation. Often, such ceremonies made it onto local television.

Bud was a former surfer and early 1970s skater from Myrtle Beach, South Carolina. Although his curly hair made him look like a surf rat, he was a businessman. His interest in skateboarding was now strictly financial.

Bud was scouting skaters during the first weekend in February. The weather had been great all winter. So it was another perfect day to jam at the park. Dane and I arrived around 11. We did the same thing we did every time we showed up at the park. We looked for Craig. Once again, he wasn't there. This time, though, in scanning the scene, we noticed Bud. He was dressed in an ugly pink and blue Hawaiian shirt. He stood out like a sore thumb. I think he wanted to.

Dane and I knew why Bud was there. So we put our game faces on and got down to business. Hot Dog was up first. He took off down the concrete, heading straight for Bud. Once in front of him, Dane did a couple of 360-degree spins. He then did a perfect *pop shovit*. After ollieing, Dane kicked his back foot behind him. This caused the board to rotate inward. Keeping his entire body straight, Hot Dog jumped as high as he could. While he stayed put, his board did a 180. He landed squarely on his deck and rode away with a smile.

"Sick!" I yelled, pumping my fist.

I noticed that Bud wrote something down in a notebook he was holding. I took this to be a good sign for Hot Dog.

While he still had Bud's attention, Dane circled around and picked up speed. Aiming for the bench Bud was sitting on, he zeroed in. Dane ollied again, turning 90 degrees onto the edge of the bench. The sight of Dane coming straight at him caused Bud to jump for safety. Lying on the ground, he kept an eye on Hot Dog Armour.

Dane then did a boardslide, grinding the bottom of his deck along the bench. He slid along the entire stretch of the seat, then turned out and landed smoothly. He rode away with both hands in the air.

If Bud was upset about having to bail, he didn't show it. In fact, he was laughing out loud as he sat back down.

I was up next. Dane had been quite impressive out there, and my competitive juices were flowing. I pushed off and picked up speed. As I did, I put my back foot on the tail and got ready to ollie. As I rose up in the air, I turned my board to the left. Next, I grabbed it really hard and fast. Using my arm and front foot, I tweaked the board out and turned it sideways. All while in mid-air.

Still airborne, I used my arm to push the board back to the right. It was back pointing straight ahead. I let go, crouched, landed cleanly and rolled away. That trick was a *nosebone,* and a textbook one at that. Bud grabbed his pencil once again.

I heard several loud whistles from the crowd. Dane was cheering the loudest. But I wasn't done yet. Not today. I was intent on showing everybody at the park that I could skate. Sure, I knew Bud was watching, and I wanted to impress him. More than anything, though, I wanted to prove I belonged, despite not being a local.

I went over to the halfpipe. I planned on nailing that pesky *noseblunt tailgrab* today. This difficult trick had given me lots of trouble in the past. I had seen Craig execute it perfectly a few times. Although Dane had attempted it, I had never seen him land one.

I went in fakie with just enough gas to get me to the top. Looking straight ahead, I locked the nose of my board on the coping. The board was now pointing toward the sky. I grabbed the tail with my left hand. Bending my knees, I pretended I was jumping off it. Of course, the board came with me. I carried it underneath me until the back trucks had cleared the coping. I crouched and landed on the transition.

Making sure Bud was watching, I made my way to the other side of the pipe. I had just landed one of the hardest tricks I could do. But I was determined to do more. My plan was to nail a second, even harder trick. In the process, I would show everyone at the park what I could do.

I kept my body centered over my board as I approached the lip. Hoping I had enough height, I executed a kickflip. Thankfully, I was over the lip when my board began spinning. Timing is everything with this trick, the dangerous *kickflip to fakie rock 'n' roll.* I didn't want to land on my board while it was upside down. Not only would I look like a spaz, but I'd also most likely crack my deck. Maybe my head, too.

My board landed on the coping correctly, between the trucks. A millisecond later, I landed on it— in correct fakie position. As I rocked, then rolled on out, I looked up. When I saw Dane clapping wildly, I gave him a crisp, Air Force salute.

It was the best move I had ever done. Man, was I stoked! So was Bud LaCross, because he came right over. As he was walking toward me, he motioned for Dane to follow him. "You boys interested in skating for The Flight Deck?" he said in his Carolina drawl.

"Both of us?" I asked. I couldn't believe it.

"Both of you," he said. "I knew the kids here in Sebastian were good. But I didn't know *how* good. You local boys can rip!"

Dane and I slapped five. I was as excited about being called a local as I was making the team. Still, I couldn't help but notice that one of us local boys was missing.

We left the park with Bud and headed over to The Flight Deck. After we picked up some free gear, we tried on our competition T-shirts. I couldn't help but chuckle as I pulled on the shirt. The words The Flight Deck were written across the front. On the back was a graphic of an aircraft carrier shaped like a skateboard. Was this a perfect uniform for a military brat nicknamed Flyboy, or what?

Dane found it rather amusing, too. He said our motto should be Aim Higher, in honor of my Air Force roots.

Bud handed us a schedule of events before we left. It included about 20 skateboarding contests. Most of them didn't take us too far away from Sebastian.

As we were looking over the dates, Bud shared

something with us. "I made up my mind when I saw the two of you skate earlier today. I'm planning on having the team compete in Orlando, at the Open in the fall."

"The Open?" said Dane. His mouth almost hit the floor. "You're kidding, right?"

"Nope."

"What's the Open?" I asked.

"It's one of Florida's biggest amateur contests," said Dane. "It's an awesome event."

"Could be good for you guys, you know, exposure-wise," said Bud.

"And great for The Flight Deck," I said.

"Yeah, I guess so," said Bud with a wink.

We smiled. Dane and I were happy to help Bud's store get publicity. We were grateful that he had chosen us. If we skated well, we could not only help our cause, but Bud's as well. Why shouldn't Bud cash in? Everyone else was.

"I hear some pros will be at the Open this year, too," said Bud. "They'll bring in the crowds *and* the cameras. They'll also attract the best amateurs in the country. All the major skateboard companies will want to see the top up-and-comers."

As Bud left to wait on a customer, Dane and I looked at each other. I'm pretty sure we were thinking the same thing. We might actually get to skate with Craig Pedersen again—or, even better, against him.

Throughout the spring and summer, Hot Dog

and I skated, and skated, and skated. We participated in just about every event held along Florida's coast. Hot Dog won the street title in Merritt Island in June. He did it again in Stuart in July. And he came in second in Palm Bay in August.

I, on the other hand, took my game to an even higher level. I took three vert titles in my first season of competitive skating. They were in Stuart, Satellite Beach and Fort Pierce. I even tied for first in the street competition, in Vero Beach of all places. Dad was there to witness that victory. Afterward, we celebrated at a Vero Beach Dodgers game. Dane came with us, too, and we had a blast.

As it turned out, Dad loved watching me skate. In fact, he tried to make it to every skateboarding event I participated in. Mom came to a few as well. But Dad was developing a true love for the sport. He now routinely read my skateboard magazines and would often stop by the skate park. The hard-nosed, strict, uptight colonel loved to watch the freedom and excitement of skateboarding! Our relationship had never been stronger.

Dad no longer pressured me about soccer—or anything else for that matter. I had gained his trust. He knew I was a good kid. My grades were excellent, and I worked hard at Dex's. Plus, I was becoming one of the top skateboarders in Florida.

A big reason for that was my dedication to practice. I'd begin my morning training sessions like any good soldier would—at 5 in the morning. Dane called me crazy, vowing never to wake up that early to skateboard. His comments didn't bother me. As other skaters slept, I was catching up to them fast.

Dane could never understand my pursuit of excellence. "You say you skate for the pure joy of it, Flyboy. But you've turned it into a job," he would say. Hot Dog couldn't have been more wrong. I'd explain to him that most people got up early for their jobs because they *had* to. I got up at 5 in the morning because I *wanted* to. There was nothing odd to me about popping an ollie as the sun came up. In fact, to me, that was the way it should be.

As I improved, I started to see the possibility of one day becoming a pro. I had never thought about it before. No, I didn't plan on making any drastic moves toward achieving that goal. And I wasn't going to pull a Grommet and start hanging out with older skaters. My plan was to stay on course. Become an Air Force pilot *and* a good skateboarder. Later on, if someone wanted to pay me to skate, I'd consider it. But for now, I focused on being the best I could be.

That summer was fantastic. Hot Dog and I were local heroes, doing our thing. And we were beginning to turn some heads.

So, apparently, was Craig—but not for the same reasons. We kept tabs on him by reading the skateboard mags and surfing the Net. He had started out strong, getting favorable reviews. But lately, he had faltered. He scored poorly in Miami, fell three times in Jacksonville and tanked it in Charlotte. A report from that competition said Craig looked "unfocused and out of sync." It said he skated as poorly as his Sebastian teammate, Eddie Rios, "a real poser."

We hardly saw Craig anymore outside of school. When we did, he didn't look like himself. He always appeared exhausted, like he hadn't slept in days. His eyes were red or glassy. He smelled like beer. Once again, I had my suspicions. I wondered if Craig was drinking all the time now.

CHAPTER ELEVEN

FALL FROM GRACE

On the drive up to the Orlando Open, I thought about my life. Just 13 months ago, I was living in Germany, getting ready for soccer season. Then, just like that, I was on a plane headed back to the United States. My destination: a town along the ocean where skateboarding ruled.

Now, I was a 15-year-old freshman at Indian River High School. Two months earlier were soccer tryouts. They came and went without me. I had hung up my cleats for good. I no longer was interested in the sport I had played since I was 6.

I had become a skateboarder. I found my true essence in this sport. And I shined brighter than I ever did on a soccer field. I was known as Flyboy, one of the best skaters in Sebastian. I was also the leader of a radical local skate team.

My father was particularly happy with my role

on The Flight Deck team. I found it easy to be a leader. The skaters looked up to me because I worked hard and never quit. It was that simple.

Nearly all of them were interested in pushing their bodies and souls, though. Every day, we cheered each other on as we attempted to accomplish the impossible. Together, we turned the unbelievable into reality and made the amazing seem routine.

Bud's minivan slowed down as we exited the freeway. I looked around and felt really good. I was truly happy with where I was in my life. Even so, there was a hole in my heart—as well as Hot Dog's. It was a hole that success on a skateboard couldn't fill. We missed our friend Craig, who seemed to be spiraling out of control.

My eyes brightened as we pulled up to the TD Waterhouse Center. The parking lot of the arena had been turned into a skate park. There were rails, ramps, pipes and pools. Obviously, no expense had been spared. My heart raced when I realized this would be my first big-time skateboarding experience.

As Dane and I went to register, we saw skaters from all over the country. This wasn't just a Florida event. There were skaters from as far away as Los Angeles and Seattle. I had actually heard of some of them. Their names and photos often appeared in the magazines I read. I wasn't intimidated, though. That's another thing about skateboarding that I loved. No matter who I was facing, it ultimately came down to me and my board.

The bleachers filled up quickly. Bud pulled out new shirts for us to wear, as well as caps. In addition to the name of his shop and his logo, he added Aim Higher! We were fully dressed in Flight Deck gear a few moments later. Good thing, too, because the first event was set to begin in 30 minutes.

Although I was excited about the competition, I didn't like all the bells and whistles. Suddenly, I felt like an outsider again. Just about everyone on the grounds was wearing a tie and talking on their cell phone. Corporate America had invaded, and there was no stopping it.

Unfortunately, Dad wasn't able to make it to the event. He had an important meeting in Miami. I understood, but I was still disappointed. I think he was twice as upset, though. I took a deep breath and remembered his advice from that morning. "No fear. No expectations. Have fun." I repeated his words in my head: *No fear. No expectations. Have fun.*

To me, just about everyone else at the Orlando Open "expected" something. The Open seemed to expose the one thing I didn't like about skateboarding. There was money to be made everywhere! If you "sold out," that is.

I put these thoughts to rest as we made our way over to the halfpipe. Then I tried to see the other side of the argument. Maybe the business of skateboarding wasn't such a bad thing. I mean, if skateboarding hadn't gone mainstream, I wouldn't have been in Orlando. In fact, I probably never would have stepped on a board in the first place. Maybe I *should* get cozy with some skateboard sponsor. You know, start thinking about a future in the sport.

"Hey, Hot Dog," I said to Dane. "Does all this glitter turn you on?"

"What do you mean, Flyboy?" Dane asked.

"All the money, the sponsors and everything," I answered.

He scratched his bushy head of hair. "It's no big deal," he said. "If skateboard companies want to throw product my way, I'm all for it. They get paid, I get paid. It's all good. It's not like I'm gonna pull a Grommet and drop my best friends, right?"

I smiled at his pull a Grommet comment. This was a saying Dane and I had started using often.

"Look at it this way, Flyboy," he continued. "I could put up with all this. If that's what I have to do to get paid to skateboard."

"I don't know," I said. "To me, it all seems to get in the way of the skating."

"Flyboy, you're too serious," said Dane, shaking my shoulders. "We're at the Orlando Open. Let loose, dude!"

I pushed Dane backwards jokingly. "Let loose, huh? You mean like *him*?" I pointed across the parking lot at Craig Pederson. He was standing alongside Eddie Rios and a few other skaters wearing Javelina apparel. They were being interviewed by a female reporter while each flirted with a pretty girl.

Without speaking a word to each other, Dane and I walked over.

"Hey, Craig," I said. I was willing to be polite while not forgetting our last real conversation. That was the one in the hallway before homeroom nearly a year ago. "Long time no see."

"Flyboy Hardin," he said. It sounded like he was slurring his words again. "What's up?"

The reporter took this as her cue to leave. Craig let go of the girl he was holding hands with and almost fell. Then he composed himself.

"Hot Dog Armour, too," he could barely get the words out. "See, I told you my boys would come to see me skate, Eddie."

"We'd love to see you skate, but that's not why we're here," I said. "We're competing."

Eddie Rios started laughing so hard he almost fell over. "You're competing?" he asked. "At the Orlando Open?"

"That's right," said Dane.

"You Flight Deck guys are small-timers," said Eddie. "This is way out of your league."

"Gotta go for it sometime," said Dane. "I think we're ready."

"That's cool," said Craig. "I hope you get picked up."

"Yeah, me too," Dane said.

I watched Craig as he swayed back and forth. There was no mistaking it. He was drunk. … again. "How about you, Toby?" he asked. "You ready for a bump up to the big time?"

"I just like skating, Craig," I answered. "I mean, it would be cool to skate professionally at some point. But if that means drinking and hanging out with Eddie, you can have it."

That stopped Eddie's laughter, but triggered Dane's.

"You're a punk, Hardin," Eddie said.

I stared into his eyes and took a step toward him. I wasn't scared of the 19-year-old. I was in great shape and twice the athlete Eddie was. Plus, I wasn't drunk. If he tried to get tough with me, he wouldn't like the outcome.

"You're just Eddie. You're nothing," was my reply. I looked over at Craig again.

"C'mon, Grommet," Eddie motioned with his hand. "I'm not wasting any more time talking to these losers."

I waited to see what Craig would do next. Would he stay and talk with us, his old friends? Or would he leave with Eddie Rios, the world's biggest jerk?

Craig looked over at Eddie and then back at me. "You know, Fl-Fl-Flyboy," he said, once again slurring, "I heard this junk from you b-before. I'm not going to listen to it again."

He turned and began to follow Eddie.

"Fine, but what you're doing to yourself is affecting your skating, if you haven't noticed." I called after him, "You used to be great, Craig."

Craig stopped. Then he stood there for what seemed like an hour. In truth, it was probably about 10 seconds.

Dane and I looked at each other and shrugged.

Finally, Craig turned around. "I'm still g-g-great," he said. What looked like a tear was coming down his cheek. "Better than you guys."

Then, he turned his back, hiccupped and walked away.

At that moment, I wasn't mad at Craig anymore. Neither was Dane. We actually felt sorry for him. He looked like he needed help. But what could we do?

"The show starts in 10 minutes," I said, slapping Hot Dog on the back. "We need to gear up."

If Bud hadn't told us, we'd never have known that the other competitors were amateurs. They were amazing. We were alongside the sport's next crop of superstars. Eddie may have been right about Dane and me being out of our league. But that was okay—at least for me. I hadn't come to Orlando to win. I came to compete, to learn and to push myself further as an athlete. *No fear. No expectations. Have fun.*

Dane was a bit disappointed, though, after his run. He thought he would have fared better. I had to tell him not to get down. I explained how there were more than 150 competitors here. I also reminded him that we were younger than most of them. The fact we were even *at* this event said something about how good we were.

I put on my pads and helmet for my run. Standing atop one side of the halfpipe, I scanned the audience. Vert skating always drew the big crowds. This was no exception. I was a little nervous standing up there, especially when the fans started making noise. My palms were sweaty and my heart was pounding.

"No fear. No expectations. Have fun," I whispered aloud. Speaking Dad's words actually worked. A moment later, I was calm and cool, ready to fly. I dropped into the pit with a burst of energy. I went through my routine of tricks, landing most of them perfectly. That was when I decided to go for it. After all, I had nothing to lose. My plan was to nail a *heelflip indy,* a trick I had only landed once. What the heck, right?

I got a good jump. As I headed into the transition, I picked up speed. By the time I climbed the other side, I was in the zone. I smacked the tail of my deck hard, then kicked my front foot out. The board floated up between my legs and near my waiting hands. Now, in a full, mid-air split, I grabbed my board with one hand. Then, I thrust it under my feet. And when I stuck it cleanly, I heard the roar of applause!

Little did I know, but my run landed me in 11th

place overall in vert! It was an incredible showing for a rookie. I never thought I'd crack the Top 25. It was due to that heelflip indy, the one trick I couldn't do all summer. In Orlando, on the grandest stage of them all, I nailed a beauty.

After my run, people started approaching me. There were a few reporters and a rep from a company I'd never heard of. Plus, a few skaters wanted to meet me. Getting respect from my peers was the best part for me. The rest of it was just annoying, because it wasn't about what I'd just done. It was business. One guy asked me whose board I used. A reporter was curious as to which pros I admired. And another wanted to know when I'd be skating next. Nobody, except for the other skaters, even knew what a heelflip indy was.

The final question made me smile, though. A reporter asked me where The Flight Deck was. I told her the answer and winked at Bud. He gave me an enthusiastic thumbs-up.

I didn't feel comfortable with this sudden popularity, though. After what had happened with Craig, I didn't trust these people. Especially the ones looking for me to sign my name on some dotted line. What I *wanted* to do was watch the finals. And that was because my former best friend, Craig Pederson, was still in it.

An hour later, Dane and I settled in to watch. Only five skaters remained. And their task was to duke it out in a 15-minute jam session. The winner would capture the overall title.

These five had been skating all-out all day, pushing the limits. As a whole, they were killing the course with some radical skating. It was obvious these guys were dog-tired. They had been at it for four hours. But they weren't holding back. They all wanted it badly.

Despite everything that had happened, Dane and I wanted Craig to win. Deep down, he was still one of us, a kid from Sebastian. It just so happened he was also the best young skater we'd ever seen.

After two of the finalists stuck their tricks, two others fell on the vert ramp. That all but eliminated them from contention. It was now Craig's turn. We watched as he stood atop the platform on the halfpipe. He didn't look nervous to us, but he did have those glassy eyes again.

"I wonder if he's still trashed," said Dane. "He sure looks it. Man, I can't believe he'd risk losing this thing for a few beers."

"What an idiot," I said. "He drops us for his career only to ruin his career by drinking? It makes no sense."

"I can't believe he made it all the way to the finals," Dane said.

"It just goes to show you how good he really is," I said. "Imagine if he didn't drink today. This thing wouldn't even be close right now."

Craig was given the green light to push off. He

did, heading down into the transition. I had a feeling he was going to try a really difficult aerial. You know, win it all in one swoop. That was just like him—and just like me, too. Be aggressive, take it to your opponent, make *him* play catch-up.

Craig flew over the coping and launched skyward. He dropped his left hand to blindly grab his board behind his back foot. He was attempting an *indygrab*. Only, he miscalculated somehow. The board wasn't where his hand expected it to be. As a result, he snatched at air while his body kept moving up and away. Immediately, I knew he no longer was going to have a skateboard to land on.

Craig had gotten so much air—*big air*—that he was well above the platform. In fact, he was still floating when his board landed in the transition, upside down. As it slid down into the pit, Craig crashed into the railing atop the platform. He hung there for a minute. And then, before several other skaters could grab him, he fell over the side.

I gasped.

"No!" shouted Dane.

By the time we got over there, the paramedics were already on the scene. We watched as they took Craig away in an ambulance, sirens blaring.

CHAPTER TWELVE

BROTHERS

The fall was at least 20 feet—onto blacktop.

As we made our way to the hospital, we speculated about Craig's fate. "He could be paralyzed," said Dane. "I heard about a skater who went over the edge. He ended up in a wheelchair."

"What if he landed on his head?" I asked. "He could be even worse than paralyzed."

"No need getting yourselves all worked up," said Bud from the front seat. "We'll find out what happened to him in a minute."

"Just think, if he hadn't been drinking, he would have won the Open," I said. "With his talent, all Craig had to do was *not* do something stupid. He could have been a champion."

"He did the stupidest thing he could think of," said Bud, as he pulled the van into a spot in the hospital parking lot.

Dane and I ran into the Emergency Room. We sprinted past a number of patients to the desk. Once there, we asked the nurse on duty what happened to Craig Pedersen.

"Who?" she asked, without looking up.

"Pedersen," I said. "Craig Pedersen."

"The skateboarder?" she asked, still not looking up.

"Yes, ma'am," I said. "They brought him in by ambulance a few minutes ago."

"Are you family?" she asked.

I looked over at Dane, who had a tear rolling down his cheeks. His face revealed his worst fears.

"We're his brothers," I said.

She looked up at Dane and me with compassion in her eyes. "I'll see what I can find out."

We sat down to wait with Bud and the rest of The Flight Deck team. Nobody spoke a word. Everyone was deep in their own thoughts. After a few minutes, the nurse came out from behind two double doors. She walked over to Dane and me. "You're brother is one lucky boy," she said.

We let out a sigh of relief.

"How is he?" I asked.

"He broke both legs, fractured a wrist, bruised a few ribs and flattened his nose. Other than that, he's pretty banged up," she said. "He's also drunk. Did you boys know he had been drinking?"

We avoided eye contact with her.

"We weren't sure, but yes," I said, staring at my sneakers. I felt guilty. "Can we see him?" I asked.

"Not tonight. He's under observation. He won't be leaving the hospital for a while yet."

With no chance at seeing Craig, we decided to head back to Sebastian with Bud.

On our way out of the hospital, I saw Eddie Rios. Bud and the rest of the team kept going. But I lingered behind. I wanted to talk to Eddie.

"Hey, Eddie," I said, anger evident in my voice.

"Oh, hey, Flyboy," he said uneasily. "I didn't see you there."

"I bet," I responded. "What are *you* doing here?"

"I came to see Craig." His voice was anxious.

"Why do you think he'd want to see you?" I asked.

"I don't know, Flyboy. Maybe because I'm his friend," Eddie said sarcastically.

I smirked. "Some friend," I said. "Got him drunk before a skateboarding tournament. Ruined his chances at winning . . . and nearly killed him!"

"That was his call, dude!"

"Yea, but you had the booze," I said.

"Look, Flyboy, I've just about had it with you."

I smiled. "That's funny, Eddie, because I've just about had it with you, too."

My body took on a different posture, as my rage started to bubble over. If Eddie was ready to throw a punch, I was ready to throw one back.

Sensing my intentions, he took a step backward. "What room is Craig in? I have to see him."

"Why?" I said. "You scared? Well, you should be, Eddie. If anyone finds out about what you guys were doing before the Open, you're toast!"

"Don't you think I know that?" he said. Then, not bothering to lower his voice, he continued. "I need to get in to see Craig. Help me, Flyboy. For Craig's sake. I need to make sure he doesn't say anything about the drinking. Especially where he got the beer from. And I need to do it before someone from the tournament shows up to investigate."

At that moment, one of the officials from the Open walked up to us. "Care to repeat that?" he asked, now joined by two other officials.

Eddie's face turned white. He was busted—big time!

"You're really something, Eddie!" I yelled. "You didn't come here to see how Craig was doing. You came here to protect yourself. You're some friend!"

After I said what I needed to say, I headed for the exit. I glanced back over my shoulder to see Eddie and the officials talking.

I heard one official say Eddie was off the Javelina team for underage drinking. I assumed that Craig would be as well.

It was a wonder they weren't kicked off the squad sooner, I thought.

At home later that night, my dad asked if I had a few minutes. He wanted to know how I was feeling about Craig. He knew about the accident—and the drinking—before we sat down. But he didn't say "I told you so."

"What do you make of this whole thing, Toby?" he asked.

"I think Craig made a big mistake," I said. "And I think he's going to pay for it for a long time."

"I agree," Dad said. "Why do you think it happened?"

"I don't know," I said.

"I do," he said. "I think Craig lost sight of what was truly important. Skating for the pure joy of it, like you do. So he turned his back on his friends, the ones who kept him flying right."

"Yeah, I guess so," I said. "*We* certainly didn't abandon him."

"No," Dad said. "But you suspected he was drinking a while ago, didn't you?"

"Yes," I answered. "I tried to reach out to him. I could have done more, though."

"You probably could have," said Dad. "Are you planning to reach out to him again now?"

"I hadn't thought about it," I said. That was the truth. I didn't know what to make of Craig's accident. I mean, we had grown so far apart. It's like we didn't even know each other anymore.

"Think about it," my father said. "He's never

needed a friend more than he does right now."

My face indicated to my father that I wasn't getting his point. He went on.

"You and Dane were his good buddies, the people he could always count on. When times get tough, we all need people to lean on. You, Airman, should understand that."

Dad was right. I remembered how I felt when we left Texas for Germany. If it weren't for Mom and Karl, I don't think I would have made it. Then, when we left Ramstein for Florida, it was Craig who I leaned on. He kept me from being miserable. He reached out to me. If he hadn't, I would have likely just sat in my room, cursing my father.

Now, skateboarding and my relationship with Dad were the best things about my life. Honestly, I owed a lot of that to Craig. I now understood what my father was talking about. When you're up, you don't need help as much. It's when you've crashed that you need the support of your friends. And, in Craig's case, his crash was every bit as emotional as it was physical.

"Yes, sir," I told my dad. "I understand."

It didn't take much to convince Dane to come to the same conclusion. Two days later, when I learned Craig was home, I got Dane on the phone. "I think we should go see Craig," I said.

"Why, dude?" Hot Dog asked. "He bailed on us."

"He didn't bail on us," I explained to Dane. "He made a deal with Eddie, thinking it'd get him where he wanted to go. Everything snowballed from there. In the end, it was a stupid mistake," I added. "But it really didn't have anything to do with us. Right now, you think he wants to see *Eddie*?" I asked.

Dane thought about it. Ultimately, it wasn't about logic and what made the most sense to him. It came down to the fact that, like me, Hot Dog missed Craig. "Fine, let's go," he said. "It's about time we got the crew back together."

We skated over to Craig's house after school. His mom answered our knock at the front door. I could tell she and Craig's dad knew about his drinking.

"Dane! Toby!" she said, her face breaking into a big smile. "It's so good to see you boys. I haven't seen you in such a long time. Craig is going to be so happy you're here." She walked us into the living room. "All his problems started when he stopped hanging out with you boys."

We made our way out to the back porch, which had been converted into a recovery room. Craig was sitting in an easy chair. We were shocked by how he looked. It was like he'd been hit by a bus. He had a cast on each leg that extended from his thighs down to his ankles. He also wore a cast on his wrist and sported a bandage across his face. Above it were two very black eyes.

"Gnarly!" Dane whispered.

"Shut up, dude," I whispered back to him.

"I look terrible, I know." Craig spoke with great difficulty. Only, this time, he didn't slur his words. He sounded like he was in a lot of pain.

"Grommet," Dane spoke up first. "You okay?"

Craig struggled to smile. "Do I look as bad as I feel?" he asked.

"Worse," Dane responded, as he and I broke into laughter.

At that, Craig managed a grin. I could tell right away he was happy to see us.

"What's up with you, Flyboy?" he turned to me. "I hear you kicked some butt at the Open? Eleventh place . . . unreal, dude."

"You taught me well," I said.

"Did I?" he asked, his lip quivering. "No, I don't think so. I didn't teach you anything. Except maybe how to act like a fool."

"Look, Craig," I said. "We don't care about what's happened. We only want you to get better and come skating with us again."

"Yeah, we're over it," Dane said.

"Thanks, guys. I don't deserve that, but thanks. I miss skating with you guys more than anything," he said. "But I'm not going to be able to get on a board for a while. Doc says like nine months or so."

"Well, we'll be here when you're ready," I said. Dane nodded.

Craig looked into my eyes, and then into Dane's.

Tears streaked down his face. "I'm sorry, guys. I'm so sorry."

CHAPTER THIRTEEN

LOCALS RULE

Anyone who's ever seen a skateboard contest knows that the best skating often happens during warm-ups. Following the same reasoning, most of the best skating—period—happens at the skateboard park. Usually, no one is there to see it but your friends.

This was the case a week later. Dane and I were tearing it up at the park one Saturday morning. It was early. The air was crisp, and we were the only ones there. Except for Craig, who had come along on his crutches.

Even though he wasn't on his board, Craig's appearance meant he was back. For me, Toby Hardin, the Texan from Germany, it was even more special. It meant that Hot Dog, Grommet and I were a team again. And that I was one of them.

Craig cheered as Hot Dog did a *streetplant,* then a *backside lip slide.* And he howled when I nailed in a *staple gun* and a *nosestall revert.*

Hot Dog's first trick that day was a lesson in fearlessness. His streetplant was worthy of being on a skateboard highlight reel. He had been practicing walking on his hands for weeks, and it showed. Riding forward, he picked up speed, then planted his hand on the ground. He grabbed the board and started taking his feet off, front foot first. He boosted off with his back foot and held his board aloft. Then, all at once, he brought his feet up to his board and froze there. After a few seconds, he dropped his body and board down at the same time. He rode away with a giant smirk on this face.

We ate it up, especially Craig, who rocked back and forth in delight.

My nosestall revert put the icing on the cake for our old friend. Known as the *trick of champions,* the key is all in the front foot. For me, a goofy-footer, that meant my right. With just enough speed, I approached the coping of the halfpipe. I did a basic nosestall. But, as I was getting ready to lock it in, I shifted my weight back. I extended the nose of my board forward to the coping. Then, while in full stall, I turned my body so the board would spin around. Keeping my weight mainly on my front foot, I slid the nose off the coping. I pivoted, thrusting the front end back around toward where I came from.

It was beautiful. In appreciation, Craig struggled to his feet to give me a standing ovation.

We were having a ball. Dane and I pushed each

other to pull off tricks we never attempted before. That was when a car pulled up alongside the entrance to the park. Out stepped a man in jeans and a collared shirt. He looked about 30 years old. After taking a quick look around, he headed straight for Craig.

Hot Dog and I didn't notice him until he'd sat down next to Grommet. In need of a break, we made our way over.

"Flyboy!" Craig called. "Why don't you go hit another nosestall?"

"What for?" I asked. "I should quit while I'm ahead, no?"

"Not today, dude," said Craig. "This guy wants to see you in action."

"Who's he?" I asked, looking at him.

"He's Jeff 'Fakie' Fager, former pro skateboarder," said Craig excitedly.

Dane and I indicated our acknowledgement. We knew of Fakie Fager. He was a local legend, having started skateboarding in nearby Boca Raton.

"I'm a rep for Swamp Skateboards now," he said, extending his hand. "I was just asking your friend here if he had heard of us. We're a fairly new company."

"I haven't," I answered, shaking his hand.

"Me neither," said Dane.

"We'll, we've heard of you," Fager said, looking my way.

"Me?" I asked in disbelief.

"We saw some video of what you did at the Orlando Open," the man said. "Pretty rad. I'd sure like to see some of the same in person."

I was surprised. This guy had come to the skateboard park in Sebastian to find *me*.

"We want to sponsor you, Toby," the man said. "We want you to skate for the Swamp team."

He pulled out a T-shirt from a bag he was carrying. It portrayed an angry alligator shredding on a skateboard.

Craig looked at me as I stared at the T-shirt. I didn't know what to do.

"Take the shirt, Toby," said Craig. "And then go show this guy what you can do."

"Yeah, Flyboy," said Dane. "This is your chance. Get airborne!"

I looked at the two of them but didn't say anything. I also didn't take the shirt. I was too busy thinking.

"It's your time," added Craig.

"No thanks," I said to Fager. His face showed a look of confusion. But the other faces there that day broke into grins. "No hard feelings," I added. "I just want to skate with my friends for now."

It was obvious that the rep from Swamp Skateboards didn't get it. And I didn't expect he would. He couldn't understand that it didn't mean anything to me to be sponsored. He probably couldn't comprehend how much I liked the team I was on now. And how I had no intention of leaving it.

"Toby," he finally spoke. "Do you know what you're passing up?"

"Yes sir," I said, looking at Craig, still covered from head to toe in plaster. "I sure do."

"It may happen someday," Craig said to the rep. But I sensed he was really speaking to me.

"Maybe, but only when the timing is right," I responded.

Craig smiled.

Fakie Fager wasn't through making his pitch, though. He decided to give it another shot. "Swamp Skateboards wants to promote its native sons here in Florida right from the start. You're one of the first skaters we've approached."

"Well, sir," I said, "I'm really not from here."

"Oh, okay," Fager said. He shook his head and shrugged.

As he walked away, Dane and Craig patted me on the back.

"It's true, you're not from here," said Grommet. "But you're definitely one of us."

"Aim higher, Airman," said Hot Dog, saluting me before hopping onto his skateboard.

"Flyboy," Craig said, "you're one local who rules."

Test Yourself...Are you a Professional Reader?

Chapter 1: Germany

What are a few of the responsibilities for a center-midfielder?

Toby and Karl became best friends. What did they have in common?

Why did Toby have a sense that something was wrong when he entered the house after soccer tryouts?

ESSAY

Toby is obviously surprised, and upset, to hear that his family is moving to Florida. How do you think you would react to the news that you and your family were moving to another country? Do you think Toby handled the situation well? Explain.

Chapter 2: Sebastian

Why was Sebastian considered to be such a great surfing spot?

What skateboarding maneuver did Alan Gelfand invent?

Toby is called a "shubee" by Craig Pederson. What's a "shubee?"

ESSAY

Early in this chapter, Toby labels Craig Pedersen and Dane Armour "scrubs." Towards the end of Chapter 2, he is amazed by their skateboarding abilities and athleticism. Have you ever misjudged someone by focusing on their appearance? Explain. Why is it important not to prejudge people?

Chapter 3: Two of a Kind

What was Toby's first job? What were some of his responsibilities at this job?

Why did Toby consider himself to be the "opposite of a skater?" How did his childhood help to enforce his negative view of skateboarding?

When did Toby first realize that he was drawn to skateboarding?

ESSAY

In this chapter, Toby writes that he's not planning on telling his dad about his growing interest in the sport of skateboarding. What have you kept hidden from your parents? Why? How did this make you feel?

Chapter 4: Flyboy

According to Toby, did the term "Locals Only" apply at the skate park? Explain.

Why was Craig willing to give Toby his board for Toby's first skate run?

What nickname did Grommet give Toby? Did Toby like the nickname? Why or why not?

ESSAY

In Chapter 4, Toby is moving closer to trying the sport of skateboarding. Name a new hobby, interest, or sport that you recently picked up. Why were you interested in this activity? How do you feel when you try something new?

Chapter 5: Basic Training

Was Toby a "goofy-footed" rider on his skateboard? What does the phrase "goofy-footer" mean?

What did Toby realize during the exact same moment that he nailed the perfect ollie?

Why didn't Toby's father want him to hang out with the skateboarding crowd?

ESSAY

Toby's dad talks about "making a difference in the world." What does "making a difference" mean to you? Describe your future plans, and how you plan on making a difference.

Chapter 6: The New World

According to Toby, why did Eddie mention the skateboarding prospect he was tracking in Melbourne?

Why was Craig confident that Eddie wouldn't leave him off The Flight Deck team?

What does Craig identify as the quickest path to becoming a professional skateboarder?

ESSAY

What reasoning did Eddie give for the tension between him and Craig? What did Craig point to as the reason that they didn't get along? Name a person in your life that you argue with. Why do you believe that you have a difficult time getting along with him/her? How could you change this relationship in the future?

Chapter 7: Permission to Skate, Sir

Everything was moving along perfectly for Toby in Florida with one exception. Detail what was going wrong.

How did Toby's father eventually find out that Toby was skateboarding?

What did Toby's father notice about his son when he watched him skate for the first time?

ESSAY

What did you think of Toby's father before this chapter? Did your impression of him change after the way he treated Toby when he caught him skateboarding? Explain.

Chapter 8: The Deal

Why didn't Toby grow his hair longer to fit in better with the other skaters?

Why did Craig stop skating and hanging out with Hot Dog and Toby?

What skateboarding team did Craig and Eddie join? Why did they move to this team?

ESSAY

Craig decides to start drinking alcohol in this chapter. Describe what happens to Craig after he drinks. Why do you think he's making a big mistake by drinking?

Chapter 9: The Outsider

Why did Toby want to make The Flight Deck team so badly?

What reasoning did Craig give Toby as to why he was still hanging around with Eddie?

Why did Toby feel like an outsider, again, after his conversation with Craig?

ESSAY

Why do you think that Craig has changed so dramatically? Do you believe he has changed for the better or for the worse? If you were in Toby's situation, would you *still* want to be Craig's friend? Explain your answers.

Chapter 10: Aiming Higher

Who was now in charge of selecting The Flight Deck's roster? Why was this person so committed to this task?

What is the "Open?" Which skater did Dane and Toby want to compete against at the "Open?"

At this point in the book, what does Toby's father think of skateboarding?

ESSAY

In this chapter, we read about the importance of practice. Toby improves because of his strong commitment to skateboarding. Why is practice so important? Can you think of any activity where practice does NOT help you to improve? Name an activity that you participate in. Do you believe that you practice enough to become great at this particular activity? Explain.

Chapter 11: Fall from Grace

Why did the other skaters on The Flight Deck Team look up to Toby?

What did Toby notice about Craig's condition when he saw him at the Orlando Open?

What was Toby repeatedly telling himself as he prepared to skate in Orlando?

ESSAY

In Chapter 11, it becomes clear that Craig has a drinking problem. He adds to this problem by making another poor decision. Why does Craig make a crucial error in judgment by trying to skate after drinking? Why is it so important not to operate any sort of vehicle, including a skateboard, while in Craig's condition? Do you think Craig was lucky or unlucky? Explain.

Chapter 12: Brothers

Why was Toby so angry with Eddie when he spoke with him at the hospital?

As it turned out, what was the true reason that Eddie rushed to the hospital to visit Craig?

Why did Toby feel that Craig had been a good friend to him, despite Craig's recent mistakes?

ESSAY

In Chapter 12, we read that "it's when you've crashed that you need the support of your friends." Detail a moment in your life when one of your friends was there for you. Also, write about a time when you were there for a friend.

Chapter 13: Locals Rule

According to Toby, what did Craig's appearance, on crutches at the skate park, mean?

Who is Fakie Fager? What job did he now have?

Why did Toby turn down Fakie's offer to skate for the Swamp team?

ESSAY

Congratulations! You have completed another Scobre Press book! After joining Toby on his journey, detail what you learned from his life and experiences. How are you going to use Toby's story to help you achieve your dreams? Additionally, what did you learn from Craig's mistakes?